DEADHEAD

The only sound in the room was the faint hiss of breath from the sleeping Remo's nostrils.

Forsythe looked at Chiun. "How can you kill a man who isn't conscious?" he asked.

"It is easy," said Chiun. His right hand, resting on the edge of the table, had grasped one of the dinner plates he had put there earlier. Holding the edge, he brought his arm forward fluidly. At the last moment his wrist snapped with an audible crack and the plate flew toward Forsythe with a speed that made it invisible.

It rotated so fast it whirred, but the whirring lasted only a split second before it was succeeded by a buzzing thunk as the dull leading edge of the plate hit into, spun against and sawed, and then slipped through Forsythe's neck. The plate, pinkened with a slick of blood, clunked off Forsythe's left shoulder and dropped to the floor.

Remo slept on.

THE DESTROYER series from Pinnacle Books

AUTHORS'
CHOICE

BEST
OF

THE DESTROYER

FUNNY MONEY

WARREN MURPHY
RICHARD SAPIR

PINNACLE BOOKS NEW YORK

Publisher's Note

This book is part of a series of scheduled Pinnacle reprints of the best of *The Destroyer*. While *The Destroyer* series, with more than twenty-five million copies sold, is among the bestselling action series of all time, it has grown in the last fourteen years into a cult book, read as much for its biting humor as for its action. Reviewers have called the books "flights of hilarious satire," "a mad parody on the genre," and "a brilliant commentary on our culture."

The Destroyer is all of that—and it's fun to read, too.

THE DESTROYER: FUNNY MONEY

Copyright © 1975 by Richard Sapir and Warren Murphy

An original Pinnacle Books edition.

First printing/February 1975
Fifth printing/May 1985

ISBN: 0-523-42417-5
Can. ISBN: 0-523-43407-3

Printed in the United States of America

PINNACLE BOOKS, INC.
1430 Broadway
New York, New York 10018

For Brian, Deirdre, and Ardath

AUTHORS' INTRODUCTION

This book introduced Mr. Gordons. He was sort of a space vehicle with only one program: survival. No matter where it would land, or what it was confronted with, this space vehicle was programmed to survive. It never did get into space, but managed to cause enormous mayhem on earth. This program was adaptable to any situation. It could not be killed. It was mindless. It had no morals nor qualms, nor any interest outside of its own survival. Mr. Gordons could take any disguise. Right now, he probably represents you in Congress.

In this book, an avid fan recognized the science fiction element, a departure from the series norm, and wrote a letter demanding Mr. Gordons never appear again. He had a point. *The Destroyer* did take a different turn. It has taken many different turns. It tries new things, and if they don't work, goes on to others. It also returns to what it was and is—the grand survivor of all series. And the authors have to admit they don't really know why. It could be the father-son relationship between Remo and Chiun, the satire, the violence, the history, or just the downright magic of *The Destroyer*.

In its fifteen years it has survived every trend in the publishing business, including the highs and the lows for action and adventure series.

—*Warren Murphy and Dick Sapir*
May 1985

UNGRATEFUL AUTHORS

The authors claim they do not know why *The Destroyer* series has thrived. If you have read the series, you know why. You have been exposed to me, Chiun, Master of Sinanju. Name one other series that has the House of Sinanju. Name one other series in which I appear. You cannot. And why not? Because I am not part of those disasters. The glory of the House of Sinanju, real assassins . . . not murderers or killers as these bits of pulp might indicate, has made *The Destroyer* series. In all humility, I am forced to say the reason is not magic, it is me.

And what do I get for making these two otherwise unemployable scribes rich beyond their just deserts? How many times is the House of Sinanju called glorious? The two of them seem to get their own books published well enough; but what about my great Tang poem, on the opening of the blossom? It is a mere twelve thousand pages in Kwuyshi meter. The public goes for big books nowadays I am told. Did either one of them help me get the poem published, although the tales of my glory pay their mortgages?

But lo. That is not even the greatest insult. The misinformation about Sinanju that appears and reappears in the books called *The Destroyer* is a painful embarrassment.

The House of Sinanju is not a collection of historical killers. Nothing could be further from the truth. The House of Sinanju is a house of Assassins, who by their selective service prevent mass murder called wars.

Sinanju is a kindly, gentle village on the West Korea

Bay, made up of those loyal to the masters of Sinanju who, through the centuries, have made sure there was enough to eat by helping kings and emperors keep order in the world.

Therefore, the House of Sinanju might best be described as seekers of peace and plenty, of food for the poor villagers of Sinanju so that we can feed our less fortunate brothers.

The authors have also portrayed Sinanju as gold hungry. Why, you must ask yourself, do I ask for gold in the training of Remo? Why? We who must make sure the poor of our village can eat, must make sure the currencies are valid. We have put away a bit for the very bad times. Therefore the money we get now for the destitute and poor will be needed somewhere in the future. This does not mean we are hoarders of gold. Surely you can see our problem. If you think we are being exceptionally cautious, you may not know that we have been stung severely in the past by governments. Kubla Khan, the first to introduce paper money, left us holding 18,327 yen in worthless paper. We still have a promisory note from Augustus Caesar.

These things the authors do not tell you about. I just have. It is good that you know the truth. If they will take paper money for these books, pay for them in that manner. Then you will not be cheated. You will be giving one form of worthless paper for another.

I am Chiun, Master of Sinanju

CHAPTER ONE

On the last day that his arms were attached to his shoulders and his spinal vertebrae still formed an unbroken, flexible column, James Castellano took down his .38 police special from the top shelf of his foyer closet.

It was in a Thom McAn shoe box, secured with heavy electrical tape that his children could not pick or bite through, even if they had discovered it in the small ranch house in the middle-income San Diego neighborhood where Castellano lived.

But the children were long gone now and had children of their own. The old tape cracked in his hands as he picked it off at the kitchen table where he sat eating a hard early summer peach and listening to his wife, Beth Marie, complain about prices, his salary, the new elements moving into the neighborhood, the car needing repairs, and of course, their not being able to afford the repairs.

When Castellano heard a pause, he would say "uh huh" and when Beth Marie's voice would rise, he would say "that's awful." The last layer of tape came off with the top of the box, uncovering a price of

$7.95; Castellano remembered the shoes as being finer and stronger than those he now paid $24.95 for.

The pistol was nestled in a bedding of white toilet paper and was caked with a Vaselinelike substance someone at Weapons had given him years before. There was a note to himself on a three-by-five card, hand-printed in old fountain-pen strokes with a blob in the corner.

The hand-printed card was a ten-step program he had written for cleaning the gun. It began with removing the sticky substance and it ended with "point it at Nichols's face and pull the trigger."

Castellano smiled reading the card. Nichols, as he remembered, had been an assistant district supervisor of the Secret Service. Everyone had hated him. Now the hate seemed somewhat obscene because Nichols had died more than fifteen years ago of a heart attack, and now that Castellano himself was an assistant district supervisor for counterfeit currency—"funny money" as they called it—he realized Nichols had not been such a hard boss. He had just been precise. Well, you had to be precise. It was a precise business.

"Uh huh," said Castellano, examining the absolutely clean barrel against the bright overhead kitchen light. "That's awful."

"What's awful?" demanded Beth Marie.

"What you said, dear."

"What did I say?"

"How awful it's becoming," said Castellano, and seeing that Step Eight called for the insertion of six bullets, he scraped around the bottom of the box until he found them.

"What are we going to do about it? These prices are killing us. Killing us. It's like you're taking a pay cut every month," said Beth Marie.

2

"We'll eat more hamburger, dear."

"More hamburger? That's what we're cutting down on to save money."

"What?" said Castellano, looking up from his gun.

"I said we're cutting down on hamburger to save money."

"Good, dear," said Castellano. In place of Step Ten, which at this date would have required digging up Assistant District Supervisor Nichols's long-dead body, Castellano flicked on the gun's safety catch and put the pistol in the inside pocket of his gray seersucker suit jacket. He would get a shoulder holster at the office.

"Why the gun?" asked Beth Marie.

"The office," said Castellano.

"I know it's the office. I didn't think you were about to hold up the Bank of America. Have you been demoted to agent or something?"

"No. It's something special tonight."

"I know it's something special. You wouldn't be taking your gun out if it weren't something special. I know I'm wasting my time even asking."

"Uh huh," said Castellano and kissed his wife on the cheek. He felt her hug him more strongly than usual and he returned the hard embrace just to let her know that the comfort of their relationship had not smothered his love.

"Bring home some samples, dear. I hear they're getting better every day."

"What?" asked Castellano.

"Oh, don't look so worried. I read it in the paper. You didn't tell me anything. You never tell me anything. I read that there's a lot of counterfeit twenties around. High-quality ones."

"Good, dear," said Castellano and kissed Beth

3

Marie warmly on the lips. When she turned to go back into the kitchen, he patted her on her ample backside and she shrieked, just as shocked as she had been when they were first married and she had threatened if he ever did that again, she would leave him. More than twenty-five years and 70,000 pats ago.

At the federal building in downtown San Diego, Castellano entered the blessed air-conditioned coolness of his office that made staying in a requirement for this hot summer day. In the afternoon, a messenger from Supplies brought him a shoulder holster and showed him how to put it on.

At 4:45 P.M., the district supervisor called to ask him if he had his weapon. Castellano said "yes," and the supervisor said, "Good, I'll be back to you."

At 7 P.M., two and a half hours after Castellano normally left to go home, the supervisor phoned again and asked whether Castellano had gotten it.

"Got what?" asked Castellano.

"It should have been there by now."

There was a knock on his door and Castellano told his supervisor about it.

"That must be it," the supervisor said. "Phone back after you have looked at it."

Two men entered his office with a sealed manila envelope. The envelope was stamped in black ink: "For your eyes only." The two men asked him to sign for it, and when Castellano signed the receipt, he saw that his supervisor had signed it, and strangely enough so had the Undersecretary of the Treasury and the Undersecretary of State also. This envelope had been around. Following proper form, Castellano waited until the two men were out of his office before opening the seal of the envelope. Inside were two small envelopes and a note. The first small envelope was marked:

"Open this first." The second warned: "Do not open without specific telephone authorization." The note from his supervisor said: "Jim, tell me what you think."

Castellano opened the first envelope at the corner and shook out a mint-fresh fifty-dollar bill. He held it in his hands. The paper felt real. The most common mistake in counterfeiting was the paper. An experienced bank teller, ruffling through stacks of bills, could spot funny money easily, sometimes even with his eyes closed. There was a feel to counterfeit, a cheap paper kind of feel because the rag content was usually deficient.

This bill felt real. He rubbed the corners of the bill against a piece of plain white paper, very hard. The green ink smeared off. This was a test not so much of the ink but of the paper. The special money paper of the United States government was not porous enough for the proper ink to dry. So far this bill looked good. In the corner of his office, underneath blowups of now-famous counterfeits—like the Hitler fifties that were so good they just let them stay in circulation—was the ultraviolet light. Many counterfeiters, in an effort to get the right feel, which would fool a bank teller, would use commercial high rag content paper.

The flaw was that commercial rag paper was made of used cloth and used cloth had been washed at least once and all detergents left traces that would show up under ultraviolet light. United States money was made with unwashed rags. New rag content.

Castellano examined this bill under the eerie purplish light which made his white shirt cuffs seem to glow. There was no shineback from the bill and Castellano knew how this group must have done it. They had bleached fresh one-dollar bills. This paper was real.

5

Doing that, though, posed a different problem for a counterfeiter. They had real paper with proper rag content but also a printing headache. Government money was printed on big sheets and cut down. But if a counterfeiter bleached individual dollar bills and then reprinted the paper in a higher denomination, the printing register would not be perfect. The printing might not be centered exactly. The back of the bill might differ in placement from the front. On this bill, the borders were perfect.

Under a magnifying glass, Castellano looked at the lines in the face of Ulysses S. Grant. The engraving lines were clean and uninterrupted, the skillful work of a master engraver, the sort of lines on valid bills. A photo plate made for an offset printing press could sometimes achieve this sort of lines, but could not print them on the slick high rag content paper he was holding. On this sort of paper, offset ink would run and smudge and blot. Obviously the counterfeiter had hand-engraved plates and as Castellano examined the bowl of the five that made up the fifty in the corners of the bill, he softly whistled his admiration. A craftsman had made this bill.

The last item he checked was the serial number. On rare occasions, a counterfeiter who had an excellent plate, correct paper, perfect register, and proper ink, would make the last common mistake. The serial numbers would be fuzzy. Those large crisp numbers on a bill somehow always got short shrift from a counterfeiter, who might even spend years engraving the rest of the plate. Castellano examined each number.

"Sonuvabitch," he said and dialed his supervisor on his office phone. "Are you happy now? It's nine thirty and I've worked five hours overtime. I've been toting around an old pistol since morning wondering what

6

I'm going to have to use it for and now I find it's an old, old trick that doesn't work on the greenest recruit. I don't need any more identification training. I'm the chief of that branch."

"So you say the bill I sent you is genuine?"

"It's as real as my anger."

"You'll swear to it?"

"You know damn well I will. You sent me a genuine. We would get these in training to trip us up. You probably got it, too. Each sample was better than the one before until they were giving you real ones to examine and you were pointing out flaws in the genuine."

"Would you bet your job on it?"

"Yes."

"Don't. Open the second envelope and say nothing over the phone."

Castellano tore open the second envelope labeled "Do not open without specific telephone authorization." Inside was another fifty-dollar bill, mint fresh. Castellano fingered the bill, glancing at the fine engraving around Grant's face.

"I've got the envelope opened," Castellano said into the phone, cradled between shoulder and cheek.

"Then compare the serial numbers and come on over."

When James Castellano compared the serial numbers on the two fifty-dollar bills, he said softly to himself: "Jesus, no."

When he reported to the supervisor's office with the two bills, he had two questions framed: Was there a mistake at the Kansas City mint? Or was America in serious trouble?

Castellano didn't bother to ask the questions. He knew the answer when he entered the supervisor's office. It looked like a command post just before launching a small war. Castellano had not seen so many weapons since World War II. Four men in suits and ties cradled M-16s. They sat against the far wall with the blank bored expressions of men controlling fear. Another contingent stood around a table with a mockup of a street corner that Castellano recognized. He often took his wife to a restaurant on the southwest corner and when one of the men at the table moved a hand, Castellano saw that the restaurant was sure enough there in miniature.

The supervisor was at his desk, checking his watch with a thin blond man who had a long reddish leather case on his lap. Castellano saw that it was sealed with a shiny combination lock.

Seeing Castellano, the supervisor clapped his hands twice.

"All right, quiet," he said. "We don't have much time. Gentlemen, this is James Castellano of my department. He is the one who will make the exchange. Until he—and no one else—signals that we have a valid exchange, I don't want anything walking out of that street corner."

"What's up?" said Castellano. His mouth tasted brassy nervous and as the coldness in the faces of these strange men impressed itself upon him, he felt grateful they were all on the same side. He hoped.

He wanted a cigarette badly even though he had given up smoking more than five years before.

"What's happened is that we have been lucky. Very lucky, and I don't know why. I am not at liberty to tell you who these men are but needless to say we are getting cooperation whether we like it or not from another department."

Castellano nodded. He felt moisture forming on

his right hand which held the small envelopes with the two bills. He wished he was not holding them. He felt the men with the M-16s staring at him and he did not wish to look back at them.

"We don't know how long these bills have been in circulation," the supervisor said. "It is just possible that if they've been on the streets any length of time, they might be a major factor in inflation. They could be making our currency worthless. I say 'could' because we just don't know. We don't know if a lot of this has been passed or if this is the first batch."

"Sir," said Castellano, "how did we wind up knowing anything? I didn't realize this was queer until I saw the duplicate serial numbers."

"That's just it. We got lucky. The forger sent them to us. This is the second set. The first set had different numbers. To prove they were forgeries, he had to produce identical serial numbers for us."

"That's incredible," said Castellano. "What does he want from us? With his plates and printing process, he can buy anything."

"Not anything, it seems. He wants this sophisticated software—computer programming—that's, well, part of our space program and not for sale. Jim, don't think I'm treating you like a child but I can only explain it to you the way it was explained to me. NASA, the space agency, says that when you send things into space they must be very small. Sometimes you have to send very complicated things into space and they have to do very big jobs. This all comes under a new discipline called miniaturization. These very small things can do very complicated things like reproduce the reactions of the retina of an eye. Okay. This program the counterfeiter wants is a close facsimile of what NASA calls creative intelligence. It's as close as

9

you can get to it anyway, unless you want to build something the size of Pennsylvania. Understand?"

"The guy who makes the fifties wants that thingamajig," said Castellano.

"Right," said the supervisor. "He's willing to swap the gravure plates for them. Twelve fifteen tonight on the corner of Sebastian and Randolph. That's the mockup of the corner. Our friends will tell you what takes place there. Your job primarily is to make sure the gravure plates are valid."

Castellano saw a gray-suited man with immaculately groomed hair at the corner of the mockup signal him with a blackboard pointer to come closer. Castellano went to the model and felt like God looking down at a little San Diego street corner.

"I am Group Leader Francis Forsythe. You will identify the plates on the corner. The man you will meet will be identifying the computer program. You will not leave the light of that corner with the plates. You will be picked up by an armored car. You are not to leave anyone's sight with those plates. Should the contact attempt to retrieve the plates for any reason whatsoever, you are authorized to kill said contact. Are you weapons-familiar?"

"I've got a .38 here."

"When was the last time you used it?"

"Nineteen fifty-three or -four."

"That's wonderful, Castellano. Well, just put it in the contact's face and pull the trigger hard and often if he tries something. Let me warn you again. You are not to leave that corner with the plates under possibility . . . no, make that probability of death."

"You'd shoot me if I disappeared with the plates?"

"With pleasure," said Forsythe and gave the street corner a tap with his pointer.

10

"Well, I wasn't going anywhere anyhow. What good would the plates be to me? I don't have access to this guy's paper source. What would I print queer on? Paper towels?" asked Castellano.

"It'll take paper towels to pick you up if you try to leave that corner," said Forsythe.

"You must be CIA," said Castellano. "Nobody else on this earth is that stupid."

"Let's calm down," said the district supervisor. "Jim, this plate process is so important it's more than just a counterfeit. It could literally wreck our country. That's why everything is so tight. Please try to cooperate and understand, okay, Jim? This is more than just another bogus bill. Okay?"

Castellano nodded a tired acquiescence. He saw the man with the red leather case come to the table. Forsythe's pointer came down on a rooftop.

"This is our primary sniper post and this man will man it. It has the least obstruction and best view. Show Mr. Castellano your weapon."

Castellano watched the fingers work the combination on the red leather case so quickly no one could get a track on it. The case snapped open, revealing a fine-tooled thick rifle barrel and a metal stock set in red velvet. There were eight two-inch-long stainless steel cartridges, each tipped with a white metal substance that appeared to have been sharpened. Castellano had never seen cartridges that thin. They were like swizzle sticks.

The rifleman snapped his weapon together and Castellano saw that the very thick barrel had a very thin opening. The tolerance in the boring of that weapon, thought Castellano, must be incredible.

"I can pop out the iris of an eye at fifty yards," said the rifleman. "This is the weapon. I saw you notice

11

the bullets. They are designed to disintegrate when they hit metal of any sort so we don't go damaging your plates or any machinery. They will kill very nicely, however. They penetrate skin and are curare tipped, so if you see a little pinprick on your contact's face, or hear a little sort of slap, you will know your man is in the process of dying. I do not need a second shot. So once I get him, don't you go running anywhere."

"Just thought you should know that he's the one who's going to stop you if you decide to move anywhere with the plates," said Forsythe.

"You make me root for the other side," Castellano said and was surprised to hear several of the men carrying M-16s burst into laughter. But when he looked over for expressions of support to accompany the laughter, the men turned away their eyes.

He was shown the street corner again, where he would stand, and given a gray felt-wrapped box.

"And don't forget. Try to keep the contact between you and the primary sniper. He's our best."

The man with the peculiar fat-barreled, thin-bore rifle nodded curtly.

"When you are sure you have the right goods, fall down," said the sniper. "Just collapse and keep the plates protected by your body."

"I'm setting up somebody for a kill?" asked Castellano.

"You're following orders," said the man with the pointer.

"Do what he says, Jim," said the district supervisor. "This is important."

"At this time in my life, I don't know if I want to be responsible for another man's death."

"It's very important, Jim. You must know how important," said the district supervisor, and James Castellano, age forty-nine, agreed for the first time in his life to participate in a killing if it were necessary.

He rode to the corner of Sebastian and Latimer in the back seat af a gray four-door sedan. One of Forsythe's men was at the wheel. The exchange item was wrapped in wire and tape and thick plastic all inside the gray felt-covered box; this was designed to give Castellano more time to look at the counterfeit plates than his contact would have to look at the computer software program for creative intelligence.

The car's back seat smelled of stale cigars and the seat cover felt sticky and the stop and go of the driver made Castellano woozy. He knew a bit about computers and the space age and what he was delivering was designed, he was sure, to enable unmanned space vehicles to make creative decisions when beyond the range of earth control.

But why would anyone want something like this? On earth it was next to useless, because any normal person had many times the creative intelligence of this program.

As the limousine passed a supermarket, Castellano abruptly realized the enormity of the mission. It was just possible that these 1963 Series A Federal Reserve Notes had already watered down the value of the entire currency. Massive use of the printing plates he was to pick up could account for the phenomenon of inflation during an economic depression. In the supermarket window, he saw the price of hamburger at $1.09 a pound and it was clear in that instant. When money is worth less, you need more of it to buy less. It was America's money itself that was becoming worthless if these bills had been passed massively.

13

And why shouldn't they have been? Who could stop them?

If the assistant director for currency of the California area of the Secret Service could be fooled, there wasn't a bank teller in the country who wouldn't accept the notes. They were so good, they *were* real. And for every counterfeit bill passed, the dollar in the Social Security check for the widow became that much less, the hamburger cost that much more, and every savings account became a little less secure, every paycheck bought less than the week before.

So James Castellano, who had not fired the .38 police special for more than twenty years, who spanked his children infrequently and then only at the overwhelming urging of his wife, prepared himself to help take a life. He told himself that these counterfeiters were daily taking away bits of lives from people who couldn't afford homes or good food because of inflation, and all those little losses of bits of lives added up to the taking of one life completely.

"Bullshit," said James Castellano and took the felt-covered box out of his pocket and rested it on his lap and did not answer the driver who asked what he had said. It was 11:52 P.M. on his watch when he got out at Sebastian and Latimer and began walking slowly through the hot muggy night the few blocks toward Randolph.

The contact would go under the name of Mr. Gordons, and Mr. Gordons, according to Group Leader Forsythe, would make the exchange exactly at 12:09:3.

"What?" Castellano had said, thinking that Group Leader Forsythe had suddenly developed a streak of humor.

"Mr. Gordons said 12:09:3, that's midnight, nine minutes and three seconds."

"What if I'm there at midnight, nine minutes and four seconds?"

"You'd be late," said Group Leader Forsythe.

So Castellano checked his watch again as he walked up Sebastian and he reached the corner of Randolph at 12:05 and with effort he avoided looking at the rooftops of the six-story buildings where the sniper was. He kept his eyes straight ahead on the restaurant where he had often eaten. Its windows were dark and a gray cat stared contemptuously from the cash register drawer on which it sat. A rickety yellow Ford with a wire-tied muffler vomiting black smoke chugged up the block with a half-dozen drunken Mexicans and one old bleached blonde calling the world to revel. The car passed on down the block and far off Castellano could hear an occasional honk in the night.

He remembered putting his .38 in the shoulder holster at the office but he could not remember now whether or not he had taken off the safety. He was going to look very foolish grabbing for a gun and then squeezing a locked trigger. What would he do? Yell "bang"? Then again, there were those experts on the rooftops and it was too late now to take his gun out and examine it. The night was hot and Castellano was perspiring and his shirt became wet, even at the waist. His lips tasted salty.

"Good evening; I'm Mr. Gordons," came a voice from behind Castellano. He turned and saw a very calm face and cool blue eyes and lips that were parted in a half smile. The man was a good two inches taller than Castellano, perhaps six foot one or one-and-a-half. He wore a light blue suit and a white shirt with a white and blue polka-dot tie that was almost fashion-

15

able. Almost. In theory, white and blue were good combinations, and in practice, a blue suit with a white shirt was very safe. But this combination of bleached white and glaring blue seemed beyond dashing and even tacky. It was funny. And the man did not sweat.

"Do you have your package?" asked Castellano.

"Yes, I do have the package intended for you," said the man. The voice lacked even a hint of regionalism, as if he had learned to talk from a network announcer. "The evening is rather warm, don't you think? I am sorry I do not have a drink to offer you but we are in an open street and there are no faucets in open streets."

"That's okay," said Castellano. "I've got your package. You've got mine?"

Castellano felt the heaviness of his breathing as if there could never be enough oxygen in the air this night. The strange man with the peculiar conversation seemed as calm as a morning pond. The courteous smile stayed affixed to the face.

"Yes," the man said. "I have your package and you have mine. I will give you your package for mine. Here is your package. They are the Kansas City Federal Reserve Notes 1963 Series E, front plate 214, back plate 108, which your country desperately needs out of the hands of counterfeiters. It is worth more than the life of your President, since in your eyes it affects the very basis of your economy which is your livelihood."

"Okay, okay," said Castellano. "Just give me the plates." The man was a daffodil, thought Castellano, and reminded himself that when he was sure he had the goods he was to fall down. He would not test his own gun. Leave it to the sniper to make this one into a dead daffodil. Well, Castellano hadn't advised him to go into counterfeiting.

16

The man held the two plates bare in his right hand. Between them was a thin piece of butcher's paper. Which meant to Castellano that the plates were already ruined from rubbing together. It would not have been possible for the contact to hold the plates together with the necessary pressure to keep them from sliding across one another without exerting so much pressure as to dull the fine engraved ridges.

And it occurred to Castellano as he gave over the felt-covered box in his right hand and took the two plates very carefully in his left that Group Leader Forsythe had not given him instructions on what to do if the plates were damaged, although if they were damaged that was as good as their being out of circulation. No one would pass a fifty with a scratch in the printing.

Taking the plates, Castellano, to assure that they would never be used again, rubbed them together hard with his left hand before he separated them to examine them. It was a foolish move, Castellano realized, seeing the scratch across Grant's beard on the front plate. It might have angered his contact. Castellano placed the front plate with Grant's head on top of the backplate with the picture of the U.S. Capitol and, with a penlight, started examining the seal. It was the J for the Kansas City Federal Reserve bank. The spokes on the seal surrounding the J were so good that Castellano again felt a surge of admiration for the craftsmanship. He heard his contact make ripping sounds with the gray felt package and thought that no matter how loudly the man opened it, there would still be plenty of time for Castellano to examine the plates. After all the man had to go through tape and wire and plastic to get to the computer program. Castellano would not let the ripping noise rush him.

17

"This program does not meet specifications," said the contact. Castellano looked up, confused. The contact held a small wheel in front of him. The heavy tape and wires and plastic dangled from his hands. The felt was shredded on the sidewalk at his feet.

"Oh, Jesus," said Castellano and waited for someone to do something.

"This program does not meet specifications," said the man again, and Castellano felt as if he were being told some abstract far-off fact that had nothing to do with their lives. Then the man reached for the plates, but Castellano couldn't return them. Even with the scratch through Grant's beard, he couldn't let those plates out of government hands. He had spent a lifetime protecting the verity of American money, and he would not give it up now.

He rammed the plates into his stomach and let himself fall toward the sidewalk. He heard an instant ping, apparently from his primary sniper with the curare-tipped bullet, but then felt a wrench crush his left wrist with an incredibly painful cracking sound and then there was a feel of hot molten metal pouring into his left shoulder and he saw his own left arm go by his face with the plates washed in a dark liquid that was his own blood and then the right shoulder socket was searing pain and that arm was under his knee as he settled back onto the sidewalk screaming for his mother. And then blessedly there was a wrenching in the back of his neck as if someone pulled a switch that ended everything. His eye caught a glimpse of a bloody shoe and then there were no more glimpses.

When the films of James Castellano's dismemberment were shown at the Treasury Building in Washington, Francis Forsythe, group leader, ordered the projector stopped and with his pointer touched the splotched hand holding two oblong metal plates.

"It's our belief that the plates were ruined in the scuffle. As most of you gentlemen know, the surface ridges of currency plates are highly critical. It is the belief of your own Treasury people that our group has ended the menace."

"But are you sure the plates are scratched?" came a voice from the darkened room. In the dark no one saw Forsythe's triumphant little grin.

"In our group, we prepare for the unexpected. Not only did we have three movie cameras with infrared light and film, we had still cameras with mirror telephoto lenses and special emulsion film that could blow up a fingernail the size of a wall and you could see the nail cells." Forsythe cleared his throat, then in a loud command, ordered a still of the plate. The screen with Castellano's hand clutching the two plates became dark and the rooms with it. Then the black outlines of an engraving plate enlarged many times filled the screen.

"See," said Forsythe. "There's a scratch across Grant's beard. Right there."

Now there was a lemony voice speaking from the dark in the back of the room. "That probably happened when Castellano took the plates," the voice said.

"I don't think we should argue over who gets credit. Let's just be grateful this menace is no longer a menace. After all, no one knew this money was in circulation until our contact, this Mr. Gordons, tried to get that space program," said Forsythe.

"How did he escape? I still don't understand," came the sharp lemony voice again.

"Sir?" asked Forsythe.

19

"I said Mr. Gordons should not have escaped."

"You saw the film, sir. Do you want to see it again?" asked Forsythe. His tone was both condescending and threatening, implying that only someone who did not know what he was doing would be so silly as to ask to see again what had been obvious. It had worked hundreds of times in Washington briefings. This time it did not.

"Yes," said the voice, "I would like to see it again. Start where Castellano takes the two plates and rubs them together, causing the scratch on Grant's beard. It occurs simultaneously with his handing Mr. Gordons that false program."

"The film again, from about frame 120," said Forsythe.

"In the 140s," came the lemony voice.

The enlarged engraving of Ulysses Grant's beard disappeared from the screen and was quickly replaced by the slow-motion movements of James Castellano offering a felt package with his right hand and taking two dark rectangular plates with his left, and there the lemony voice noted drily:

"Here he scratches the plate."

And when Castellano examined the front plate under his penlight, the voice noted again:

"And now we see the scratch."

Mr. Gordons's little smile remained as he tore open the package, first on the right, then on the left, without haste but certainly without difficulty and in its slowness it still took only five seconds to have the package open.

"What did you wrap that package with?" asked the lemony voice.

"Wire and tape. He must have had some sort of

cutters or pliers in his hand to cut through the package like that."

"Not necessarily. Some hands can do it."

"I've never seen hands that could," said Forsythe angrily.

"That hardly precludes their existence," came the calm lemony voice, and a few guffaws cut the smothering solemnity.

"What'd he say?" hissed another voice.

"He said just 'cause Forsythe never saw it, doesn't mean it ain't."

There was more laughter, but Forsythe pointed to Mr. Gordons dismembering Castellano, first left arm, then right arm, then snapping off his neck until only a trunk writhed on the bloody sidewalk.

"Now tell me he didn't have an implement in his hand," Forsythe demanded, addressing the room in general, but clearly challenging the lemony-voiced man in the rear.

"Roll back to the 160s," said the lemony voice and at frame 162, as the slow-motion film rolled, Mr. Gordons began taking apart Castellano again.

"Stop. There. That little small tear in the forehead of Mr. Gordon. That's it. I know what that is. It's one of your little bullets with the poison in it, isn't it? The one you use where machinery or things you don't want damaged are involved. Correct?"

"Uh, I do believe that was a function of our primary sharpshooter, yes," said Forsythe, boiling because the weapon's existence was supposed to be supersecret, known only to a few persons in government.

"Well, if it worked and the man was hit and is poisoned to death, how is it that we see him in the 240s frames, running away with the plates?"

A few people coughed. The brightness of someone

21

lighting a cigarette broke the darkness. Someone blew his nose. Forsythe was silent.

"Well?" said the lemony voice.

"Well," Forsythe said, "we are not sure about everything. But after a long time of our currency being diluted without the Treasury people even knowing it, we can be delighted with the fact that the plate has been damaged beyond further use. The menace has been ended."

"Nothing has been ended," snapped the lemony voice. "A man who can make one set of perfect plates can make another. We haven't heard the last of Mr. Gordons."

Two days later, the Secretary of the Treasury received a personal letter. It asked for a favor. The sender wanted a small space program concerning creative intelligence. In return for it, he would give the Treasury a perfect set of printing plates for hundred-dollar bills. To prove it he enclosed two perfect hundred-dollar bills. That they were counterfeit was proved by the fact that both bore the same serial numbers.

The note was from Mr. Gordons.

CHAPTER TWO

His name was Remo and he moved easily in the predawn darkness of the alley, each movement a quiet, precise, yet quick going forward, gliding past garbage cans and pausing briefly at a locked iron gate. His hand, darkened by a special paste made of beans and burned almonds, closed on the lock of the gate. With a weak groan the gate opened. His hand silently deposited the cracked lock on the pavement. He looked up. The building rose fourteen stories to the black-gray sky. The alley smelled of old coffee grounds. Even behind Park Avenue in New York City, the alleys smelled of coffee grounds, just as alleys did in Dallas or San Francisco or even in the Loni Empire of Africa.

An alley was an alley was an alley, thought Remo. Then again, why shouldn't it be?

His left hand touched brick and moved upward, feeling the texture of the building's side. Its ridges and crevices registered in a far deeper place than his consciousness. Now it required no more thought than blinking. In fact, thought detracted from the greater power of a person. At the time of his training he had been told this, but he could not believe it; after many years of training, he gradually had come to understand. He did not know when his body and, more importantly, his nervous system had begun to reflect the change in his mind, making him something else. But one day he realized it had happened long ago, and then that which had once been a conscious goal was now done without much thought.

Like climbing a smooth brick wall that went straight up.

Remo flattened his face and arms to the wall and moved his lower trunk in close and let his legs be loose and then with the easy grace of a swan pressed into the wall and raised his body by lowering his hands with great pressure on the wall and when his hands were down near his waist, the inside of his large toes touched a brick edge, securing and resting, and the hands went up again.

He could smell the recent sandblasting of the wall. When they were old and uncleaned, walls absorbed very heavily the auto fumes of the street. But when they were clean, the fumes were very faint. The hands floated up and then down and catch with the insides of the big toes and then up.

It would be a simple job tonight. In fact, it had almost been cancelled by an urgent message from upstairs about a currency problem and would Remo look at some films of a man being dismembered and tell upstairs if the man was using some hidden weapon or if it were some special technique. Remo had said that his teacher, Chiun, the aged Master of Sinanju, would know, but upstairs had said there was always a communications problem when dealing with Chiun and Remo had responded:

"He seems very clear to me."

"Well, frankly, you're getting a little bit fuzzy too, Remo," was the lemony response, and there was nothing to answer. It had been more than a decade now and maybe he was sounding a bit unclear. But to the ordinary man, a rainbow is only the signal that a shower has ended. To the wise, it means other things. There were things Remo knew and his body knew that he could not tell another Westerner.

His arms floated up and caught a piece of loose brick. He filtered it down through his hands, not thinking of the object falling to the alley below but thinking of himself and the wall as one. He could not fall. He was part of the wall. Down went the arms, catch with the toes, up with the arms, press in and down.

The training would have changed any man, but when Remo had begun his, he had just come from being electrocuted, one of the last men to die in the New Jersey electric chair in Trenton State Prison. He had been Newark Patrolman Remo Williams, convicted of murder in the first, fast and with no pardons, with everything on the side of harsh law working perfectly, until the electric chair that was fixed not to work, and he awoke and was told a story about an organization that could not exist.

The organization was called CURE, and to admit it existed would be to admit that America was ungovernable by legal means. An organization set up by a soon-to-die President that made sure that prosecutors got the proper evidence, policemen taking bribes were somehow exposed, and in general retarded the avalanche of crime against which a gentle and humane constitution of liberties had seemed helpless. It was to be for just a little while. An organization that

25

did not exist would use for its enforcer a man who did not exist, a man whose fingerprints had been destroyed when he died in the electric chair.

But it had not been just a little while. It had been more than a decade and the training had done more than make Remo Williams an effective enforcer. It had made him a different person.

Toes catch. Not too much pressure. Arms up, down, toes catch.

"Hey, you," came a young woman's voice. "You there on the frigging wall."

The voice was to his left, but his left cheek was against the brick, and to turn his head toward the voice could plummet Remo immediately back down to where he came from. Way back down.

"Hey, you on the wall," the voice repeated.

"You talking to me?" asked Remo, listening very carefully to hear if that metal in her hand had the hollow barrel of a gun. It would have surprised him if it did. Her voice lacked the vocal tension of one carrying a killing instrument. A circle of light brightened the wall. The metal he had sensed in her hand was a flashlight.

"Well, of course you. Is there anybody else on the wall?"

"Please state your business," said Remo.

"What're ya doing on the wall already at four o'clock in the morning, twelve stories up?"

"Nothing," said Remo.

"You coming to rape me?"

"No," said Remo.

"Why not?"

"Because I'm going to rape someone else."

"Who? Maybe I know her. Maybe you won't like her. Maybe you'll like me better."

"I love her. Madly. Desperately."

"Then why don't you take the elevator?"

"Because she doesn't love me."

"Naah, I don't believe that. You've got one tremendous kind of body in that black leotard. Thin. But really nice. What's that black stuff you got over your hands? C'mon, turn around. Let me at least see your face. C'mon. Be a sport. Show it."

"Will you leave me alone then?"

"Sure. Why not? Show it."

Remo side-glided with both feet inside gripping and hands pressing to a ledge where his right hand bracketed securely, and he let his body swing out from the wall, turning his face and squinting in the flashlight beam.

"Here you are," said Remo. "Enjoy, enjoy."

"You're beautiful. Gorgeous. I can't believe anyone's that beautiful. Look at those cheekbones. And those brown eyes. Sharp lips, even with that black stuff on your face. And look at those wrists. Like baseball bats. Wait there, I'm coming out after you."

"Stay there, stay there," hissed Remo. "You can't come out here, You'll fall. It's twelve stories."

"I watched you. It's easy. Like a butterfly."

"You're no butterfly."

"If you come here, I won't come there."

"Later."

"When?"

"When I'm through."

"When you're through, you might not want to."

"I'm not really here for rape."

"I didn't think so. Maybe you'd want to date me."

"Maybe," said Remo. "But the greatest loves are always unfulfilled. With strangers who pass in the night."

27

"That's beautiful. Is that for me?"

"Yes. Go back inside, shut the window, and go to sleep."

"Good night, honey. If you need me, it's room 1214."

"Good night," said Remo and saw the light go off and the fat face go inside and the window close. He swung back to the wall. In went the feet and up went the hands. At the thirteenth floor, he sidled right again, this time lifting himself to the ledge and opening the window. The apartment appeared empty as upstairs had told him it would be. He did not have to search all the rooms. He leaned against the wall, slowing his breathing and then his heartbeat, and when he felt tensionless again, he went back to the window and swung up one more ledge to the fourteenth floor. The window to that penthouse apartment was locked. Remo eased the wood by pressure of his thumbs against the lock and then slid up and through the window. He slipped into the room and onto a soft rug. A large mound under a light white blanket snored loud enough to rumble the bowels of a cave. Behind the large mound was a smaller mound with blond hair on top.

Remo moved quietly to the larger mound and gently lifted the blanket. He rolled up the pajama bottoms, exposing two white fat hairy legs. From his dark waistband, he took a fat roll of heavy packaging tape. With one fast stroke, he had the legs wrapped securely. The legs twitched as the owner of them came awake, but before he could make a sound, Remo glided his right hand under the fat back and jammed up a thumb, pressed a spinal nerve, and the big mound of flesh quivered a bit, then stopped, and Remo smoothly slapped the big body into the air with his right hand,

28

carried it to the window, and slowly let it out on the end of the tape, like a fishing lure on the end of a line. When the fat man had been lowered nine feet, Remo laced the other end of the tape around an in-wall cooling unit, anchoring the body. Silently and quickly.

Then with his left arm on the sill, he was out the window himself, guiding with his left hand, and catching himself on the sill of the thirteenth floor apartment, one story down. Remo slid into the room, then looked outside at the very large gray-haired head, whose upside down face was turning very red. The man was conscious.

"Good morning, Judge Mantell," said Remo. "I represent a concerned citizens group that wishes to discuss your approach to jurisprudence."

"Uhhhh, uhhhh, Thelma," the voice gasped.

"Thelma is upstairs asleep. You are one flight down, hanging by your feet over thirteen stories of empty space. You are hanging by a tape. I am a tape cutter."

"Oh. What. Oh. Please. No. Oh. What."

"Our group wants to congratulate you for the courage of your convictions. Or actually, lack of them. When it was publicly noted that you had presided over 127 narcotics cases in the last two years, finding only two guilty, and you gave those suspended sentences, you declared to the press that you would not let public pressure force you to find the innocent guilty. Is that correct?"

"Uhhh, yes. Help me out of this." Judge Mantell's two arms reached for the ledge. Remo pushed them away.

"Don't do that," said Remo. "The tape is slipping."

"Oh, God, no."

"Afraid it is. But back to important matters. You

29

have a case coming up, a Joseph Bosco, or Bisco, or something, I'm not too good on names. He faces life because a young Puerto Rican pusher identified him as a main source."

"Not enough evidence," groaned Mantell.

"Oh, but there is," said Remo and he pushed down gently on Judge Mantell's chin.

"It's mandatory life," said Mantell. "Mandatory. I can't convict on just a kid's sayso."

Remo pushed again, this time harder. From the light blue pajama bottoms, a wet stain began to surge, downward toward the pajama tops and then, liquefied, along Judge Mantell's neck, up to his ears, and then into his hair and then in drops a long way downward.

"But this Bosco or Bisco already has expressed enough confidence in you to have his lawyer waive a jury trial," said Remo. "Now wouldn't a rich judge, a very rich judge like you living on Park Avenue, seem to have enough stature and self-confidence to know who is guilty and who isn't?"

"The guinea's guilty as sin," gasped Judge Mantell. "Get me out of here. Please. Guilty, guilty, guilty."

"All right. Do what I say. I want you to remember a picture. You will remember this picture every time a heroin case comes before you and someone offers you one of those fat envelopes you like so much. I know you'll have many times to remember, because half the major heroin busts in this city are already on your calendar, Judge. Lift up your head."

Judge Mantell pressed his chin against his chest.

"No. The other way," said Remo and the judge let his head drop backward.

"Open your eyes," said Remo.

"I can't."

"You will."

30

"Oh, God," moaned Judge Mantell.

"Now, if I were to drop you, your death would be infinitely easier than the death of the white powder," said Remo and he gave the tape a litttle jerk and saw the judge's arms fall above his head and he knew Mantell had fainted. He yanked the man into the room and snapped the tape free and massaged the flesh-encrusted spinal column to bring the judge back to consciousness.

Remo steadied the man on his feet.

"I will remember that alley down there, looking down at it, as long as I live," gasped the judge.

"That's nice," said Remo.

"But I may not live too long. My bodyguard, Dom, is not exactly a bodyguard. He's my executioner."

"I knew you had a bodyguard which was why I didn't come in the front way," Remo said.

"He's there to make sure I don't make mistakes," Mantell said. "The carrot and the stick. The money's the carrot; Dom is the stick."

"He has a room in your apartment?"

"That's right," said Judge Mantell, shaking.

"Breathe deeply," Remo said. "I'll be back in a minute. Breathe to the base of your spine. I don't want you dying of shock now that you've gotten religion. That's it. To the spine. Imagine your lungs are attached to your spine."

The portly judge, in urine-soaked pajamas, breathed the way he was told and miraculously he felt the terror ease away. He barely noticed the thin young man leave the empty apartment beneath his own and he was so relieved to feel the terror flood away with each exhale that he did not mark time. It seemed like only an instant and then the young man was back, guiding the huge bulk of Dom who was a good foot taller and

31

a good hundred pounds of raging muscle bigger than the thin man. But the man apparently was more bored than struggling as he guided Dom into the apartment.

"Is this Dom?" asked Remo, one hand on the back, the other on a shoulder.

"Yes, that's him," said Judge Mantell. "That's Dom."

"Goodbye, Dom," said Remo and propelled him to the window where Dom spreadeagled his feet, one on each side of the window, bracing his huge bulk. Unfortunately for Dom, this huge bulk cracked on through his pelvis and out into the open air over the alley with his feet nestled beside his shoulders. He went with a thwack and landed with a whoomph.

"I know you won't forget who we are and what we want of you," said Remo to the man in the stained pyjamas. Remo waited until he left to walk back upstairs, before going into the bathroom of the empty apartment to wash the black substance from his face and hands. He took off his black shirt, turned it inside out, exposing its white lining, rebuttoned it and left the apartment, a man in white shirt and black pants, who skipped down thirteen floors of stairs whistling, and walked out past the doorman with a cheery good morning.

He walked back to his hotel, a morning stroll along Park Avenue. When he reached his temporary suite in the Waldorf Astoria, he did his morning exercises with the heavy breathing and hoped that the frail old Oriental figure curled on a mat in the living room portion of the suite was asleep. It was Chiun's ability to place his sleeping mat in such a way as to dominate and interrupt any other activity in the room. No matter how large the room, the wisp of a man with white

32

strands of beard could always dominate it. Even in his sleep.

Only this morning he was not asleep.

"If you must do your breathing improperly, why do it where people can hear you?"

"I thought you were asleep, Little Father."

"I was. But discord shattered my peace."

"Well, if you'd sleep in the bedroom like anyone else, you wouldn't be awakened by my breathing."

"No one can be like anyone else for no one truly knows anyone else. He can be like he thinks someone else is, but not knowing what that person is, he must naturally be less. Now the someone else I am around most of the time is you, and for me to be less than you is clearly impossible. Therefore, I sleep here."

"Thanks," said Remo, who had not followed that one at all, and then he noticed a torn box on top of the television. Dark film, twisted in matted circles, rose from it like the head on a beer. The box was addressed to Remo's suite and had been hand-delivered, Remo knew, because it had the blue tag on it. The blue tag also meant something else.

"That box has the blue tag, Little Father," said Remo.

"Yes, you're correct," said the Master of Sinanju, rising in his yellow sleeping robes. "It is blue."

"And you know that blue, that color blue with the triangle shape is from upstairs, don't you?"

"From Emperor Smith," said Chiun, referring to their common boss, Dr. Harold W. Smith, the man with the lemony voice who was head of the secret organization CURE.

To Chiun, since Smith ran the organization, then he was emperor. It made no difference that Smith's ostensible title was Director of Folcroft Sanitarium.

For generation upon generation, Chiun and his predecessors, earlier masters of Sinanju, had rented their services to emperors to support the little village of Sinanju in Korea, just south of the Yalu River. Some of these emperors called themselves kings, ethnarchs, patriarchs, czars, princes, priests, and directors of sanitariums. Or even "upstairs," as Remo called Smith. But an emperor was an emperor, and he who paid the House of Sinanju was an emperor.

"I know the blue tag is from Smith. It means the box is for me alone. You are not to open it. You know that," said Remo.

"It rattled," said Chiun.

"The blue tag doesn't mean that you're not supposed to open it unless it rattles. It means that you're not supposed to open it. Rattle or no rattle."

"What difference does it make? It was broken anyway. It was all broken. When it plugged in, there was no picture. Just a light and whirring."

"It's not a television, Little Father. It's a movie projector with film," snapped Remo.

"That they forgot to put on the blue tag. But that I shouldn't open it, oh, that is important. Who sees what, that is important; but what it is does not matter. Who can understand the white mind?"

"That's the film Smitty wanted me to look at."

"Is it a beautiful story of love and devotion?" asked Chiun, his hands with long delicate fingernails coming to rest upon each other in front of him, like beautiful birds settling in their nests.

"No. Actually, it's some sort of a personal attack, one on one, with dismembering or something. Smitty wants the technique. He told me he had seen this somewhere and it was important. Something to do with money."

34

"Money for us?"

"No. Counterfeit bills."

"When you do not deal in gold, it is all counterfeit. I never trusted these pieces of paper and as you know I do not allow my moneys to the village to be given in paper. Gold. All else is a hope or a promise. Remember that, Remo. Sometimes jewels. But you do not know jewels."

Remo examined the box and began the laborious process of untangling the film and stretching it the length of the room and back until it was all out flat on the floor where he could roll it back onto the spool. Chiun watched, careful to see that none of the film touched his mat or his television set which had the daytime dramas he so loved.

"Why would anyone want to watch someone at work?" Chiun asked. "I do not understand this, although I sometimes see it on the television and naturally turn it off. Why would not Smith send you beautiful pictures?"

"It is work. He wants to know something about technique."

"Ah, that is why he is coming here this morning."

"He's coming? Why didn't you tell me?" asked Remo.

"Because the phone call didn't have a blue tag, heh, heh, heh," said Chiun and cackled intermittently until the projector was set up and running. They watched one man come to the street corner and wait. Another approached. Chiun noted the show could use organ music although he didn't particularly want to hear what they were saying. Remo said the man with the little smile seemed to have very, very good control of his breathing. Chiun thought Rad Rex of *As the Planet Revolves* was more handsome. Remo thought

35

the man had fine balance. Chiun said he couldn't wait for the commercial. Remo pointed out that something small struck the attacker in the forehead and tore at the flesh. Chiun thought that sort of thing was a disgrace to show on movies. Remo noted that the balance of the man was somehow wrong. Chiun thought the whole show lacked the feminine touch: "What is art without woman?" Remo wondered how the man did the dismemberment, feeling a respect for the victim who apparently had attempted to hold on to the objects in his hands with his last bit of life. Chiun thought the show could have used a doctor, or at least an unwanted pregnancy.

But when the film was over, Chiun was silent, staring at the blank spot on the wall where the pictures had flashed.

"Well, Little Father?" said Remo.

"I have never seen his school before. It is none of the newer fashions like Karate or Kung fu or the other game variations of Sinanju."

"What would you say it is?"

"I would say we say nothing to Smith," said Chiun. "That man is not a game. That man is real and I have never seen his technique."

"I got the feeling," said Remo, "that the things he was doing shouldn't have worked. We know how the body moves. What he did was, well, it didn't have the flow of life."

"You must avoid this man for the time being."

"Why?" asked Remo, very concerned.

"Do you know him?"

"No."

"Do you know his technique?"

"No."

36

"Then what makes you think he will not prevail over you?"

"He moves too slow. I can take him. I can take anyone but maybe you, Little Father."

"Have I taught you nothing? Does the dog attack the lion? Does the snake attack the mongoose? Does the worm attack the bird? How do you know you are not the worm or snake or dog if you do not know for sure who he is or what he is?"

"He's slow."

"An avalanche can be slow. A wave can be slow."

"Ahhhh, crap," said Remo, spinning away in frustration.

"Once again we hear the wisdom of the West," said Chiun.

When Smith came that afternoon and explained the danger of perfect counterfeits and the possibility that the entire country could go under with people literally starving to death in the street, Remo was just grateful that Dr. Smith asked only one question about the contact's technique.

"No," Remo said. "Chiun didn't recognize it."

"I sat in on a meeting, and the man who had been in charge of the abortive exchange said he thought the contact, this Mr. Gordons, had some sort of sharp instrument," said Smith in the lemony voice that matched his gaunt, parched lemony face on which a smile would appear as a foreign body.

Remo shrugged.

"But no matter," said Smith. "There are now four engraving plates. The fifty-dollar bill and this new hundred-dollar bill. I want them, and I want you to find out if there are any more. This may be the most crucial assignment you've ever had."

"Yeah. It has to do with money," said Remo.

"I don't understand your negative attitude."

"That's because you never had one."

"A negative attitude?" asked Smith.

"No. Any attitude at all. Those computers at Folcroft are the soul of this organization. We just work for those machines."

"Those computers are necessary, Remo, so that we don't have to use people. It would be impossible to keep an organization secret if thousands knew of it. With the computers, we have the perfect information coordinators. The information gatherers? Well, they're people who don't really have to know what they are doing. Most people in ordinary life don't know how their jobs fit in anyhow."

"Do we?"

Smith cleared his throat and adjusted his briefcase on his lap.

"We have a contact point for Mr. Gordons. Group Leader Francis Forsythe of the CIA is working with Treasury on this. He is expecting a special agent whose name is Remo Brian and your identity papers and credit cards are here with me now. We don't have time for our usual closed drops on identity papers. Go in and get this thing cleared as quickly as you can. In the past, I have complained occasionally about the excessive violence you have used. This time, things are so dangerous that I don't think there could be such a thing as excessive violence."

"Sure," said Remo. "We're protecting the almighty dollar. God forbid we should exert ourselves to protect an American life."

"We are protecting American lives. At every dinner table," said Smith. On his way out he paused to assure Chiun that the annual gold tribute had been transferred to the village of Sinanju in North Korea.

"The village of Sinanju places its trust in Emperor Smith and the Master of Sinanju shall always assure his glory."

"By the way, did you happen to see the films?" asked Smith.

"It is a beautiful day here in your fair New York City, no?" said Chiun and appeared calm as a white cloud as Smith attempted to unravel the answer, shrugged, and gave up, bidding the Master of Sinanju good fortune in his continued training of the American.

"Why didn't you tell him you had seen the film?" asked Remo when Smith was gone from the suite.

"For the same reason you are doing Smith's bidding against my wishes."

"And that reason is?"

"The less an emperor knows about our business, the better. We go together. I have put too much of value into your life to let you squander it," said Chiun and folded his hands again.

"You mean you're worried about something?"

Chiun did not answer.

"Are you worried about Smith?" asked Remo. "You gave him a dodge-job of an answer. You didn't want to answer him about that film. Is there something on that film that you're worried about?"

But Chiun, the latest Master of Sinanju, the grand and ancient house of assassins, was silent, and silent he remained for the rest of the day.

CHAPTER THREE

Group Leader Francis Forsythe, in khaki bush jacket and pearl gray ascot, rapped the pointer on a three-inch-high airplane hangar, which was part of a mockup of Chicago's O'Hare Airport, put together window by window, swinging door by swinging door, hangar frame by hangar frame, in a sealed Washington basement of the Treasury Building.

A sharp overhead beam illuminated in yellow artificial sun the runways, terminals, even miniature passenger jets. Round circles, ranging from light pink to dark blood red, covered the airport. Dark red at the passenger terminals and ticket counters, light pink on the runways.

"We have blood-coded the airport," said Forsythe, "so that should sniper fire go awry in our attempt to get Gordons, we will hurt as few innocent bystanders as possible. Darker red is for heavier people concentration and lighter pink is for less. Now that you see this you will understand our fire patterns for tomorrow's exchange. Our primary, secondary, and tertiary sniper stations will be cross matrixed on an evolving plane on nothing darker than pink. Maximum, pink . . . if that's all right with Remo Brian."

"How can it be all right?" asked Remo. "I haven't understood a word you said."

"I'm talking about fire patterns, Mr. Brian," said Forsythe, with enough bitterness in his voice to pucker the walls. The bitterness had been there since Forsythe had checked with his commander in Langley, Virginia, earlier in the day and discovered that this boor, who walked around in slacks and an open-necked sports shirt and who did not carry a gun, and who seemed more interested in the opinion of a senile, decrepit Oriental than in the most modern technology of counter-espionage, was—for this mission—Forsythe's superior. The order came from so high up even Forsythe's superior wasn't sure where it had originated.

"Fire patterns, Mr. Brian. I am talking about fire patterns, if you know what they are."

"That's guns going off, right?" said Remo. Chiun's delicate long fingers glided out to a miniature 747 on the airport mockup. He moved it down a runway to see if the wheels worked. With his hands, he glided it off the runway and then down over the hangar and back into a perfect landing.

Group Leader Forsythe watched. His neck reddened. He turned back to Remo.

"Correct. Fire patterns are guns going off. Now you know what a fire pattern is."

There was a smothered chuckle at the end of the table away from Remo and Chiun.

"No," said Remo. "No guns going off. None of that dilly ding-dong stuff. I don't like the idea of you people walking around with guns in the streets among citizens."

"I don't think you realize how dangerous we believe

41

this Gordons may be," said Forsythe. "More importantly, he has access to perfect plates for fifty- and hundred-dollar bills that could literally destroy our economy. I don't know what your instructions are, sir, but mine are: A, get the source of those plates and destroy it; B, get the plates themselves; and C, get Mr. Gordons."

"You have new instructions now. Stop using the alphabet," said Remo. "Now I'm supposed to give Gordons something tomorrow in exchange for those plates."

"It's being pre-processed," said Forsythe.

"What does that mean?" asked Remo. Chiun glided a Pan Am 747 into a TWA 707. Then he skirted the 707 around a hangar and back into the 747, nose into wing.

Forsythe cleared his throat and forced himself to look away from the kimono-clad old arms that were now rearranging the model planes in front of a model passenger terminal.

"What we're using as bait and what Mr. Gordons has asked for is a highly sophisticated piece of software. That's a computer program. It has to be duplicated so it won't be lost."

"It's pretty valuable, huh?"

"Not to anyone but NASA. That's the strange thing about it. This Mr. Gordons wants something that's virtually unnecessary within a few hundred thousand miles of earth."

Forsythe's voice softened. The minor coughing disappeared from the back of the room. Chiun stopped playing with the planes. Forsythe continued.

"What he wants is a computer program for an unmanned vehicle, a highly sophisticated and recent program. We and the Russians, especially the Russians, who have done more unmanned research, were getting signals back from spacecraft, a day or two days after the craft had ceased to exist. That's how long it takes for some signals to return. Naturally that means that control from NASA Houston or the Russian base is impossible in case of a real unforeseen emergency. The point is that these spacecraft just can't think. You can program them to cope with almost anything, but when something comes up that's not in their program, they can't improvise. They have no creative intelligence. A five-year-old human being would overwhelm them. The ability to see an elephant in a hunk of clay, the ability to do what our ancestors did and stick a rock on a piece of wood and invent an axe, even though they had never seen one before, is beyond them. That's what these space vehicles lacked and that's why they perished. And they couldn't call on our human intelligence back here on earth because by the time the signals got here, the whole thing was academic."

Remo felt a nudge from Chiun.

"He thinks human intelligence is all between the ears. What superstitions," said Chiun.

Forsythe rapped the pointer on a runway.

"Would your friend care to share that with the rest of us?" he asked.

"No, he wouldn't," said Remo.

There was a moment's silence, then Remo said, "So the program Gordons wants is one that is of no value to anyone on earth."

"Right," said Forsythe.

"So when you went to make the switch the last time, you gave him a phony program," said Remo.

"Right," said Forsythe.

"Why?" said Remo.

"We don't want just anybody having access to our nation's secrets. It would compromise our national honor."

The only sound in the room was Chiun snickering as he turned back to the model airplanes.

His face red under its thin coating of sweat, Forsythe said, "I'd like to suggest again that you employ snipers."

"No, again," said Remo.

"Then perhaps one man," said Forsythe and a red leather case came onto the mockup. It opened and a fat barrel with a small bore snapped into a metal lock. A hand underneath the light held forth a long thin bullet.

"I can hit an eyelash with this at a hundred yards. One hit is a kill. It's poisoned."

"You hit Mr. Gordons and he still had enough left to tear apart that poor guy you set up," said Remo.

"That was a Treasury agent and he expected to risk his life," said Forsythe, stiffening in a military manner, the pointer snapping up under his arm like a riding crop. Remo gave him a baleful look. The sniper pushed his special bullet farther down the mockup toward Remo. Into this came Chiun.

"Ratatatatatatat," he said, strafing the main passenger terminal with an American Airlines DC-10 in his left hand. With his right, he brought up the Pan Am 747.

"Zooooom," said Chiun as the 747 climbed like a fighter and chased away the DC-10. "Ratatatatatat," said the Master of Sinanju. "Varooom. Booom. Boooom. Varooooom," and the DC-10 spun crazily over the mockup of O'Hare Airport in the basement of the Treasury Building.

"Balloooooom," said Chiun when the DC-10's nose

44

hit a hanger. He let the model plane drop to the runway.

"Are you through playing with toys?" asked Forsythe.

"In your hands," said Chiun, "and in the hands of your followers, everything is a toy. In my hands, everything is a weapon."

"Very nice," said Forsythe. "I suppose now you two will take these model planes to the meeting with Mr. Gordons tomorrow at O'Hare."

"In my hands or in the hands of this man," Chiun said, motioning to Remo, "everything is a weapon, a greater weapon than that gun with your man. That gun is a toy."

"I've had enough," said Forsythe. "This is ridiculous."

"You're outa your goddam head, dink," said the sniper and his face appeared out of the darkness under the light—cold watery blue eyes behind rimless spectacles.

"Load your toy gun," said Chiun.

"Stop it. This instant," said Forsythe. "This instant. This is an order. Brian, you've got to stop your man from needling my sniper."

"I don't get involved," said Remo.

"Load your toy gun," cackled Chiun and the little DC-10 seemed to float into his right hand and come up to his shoulder. Its nose and cockpit pointed at the sniper. The sniper put the bullet into the chamber. Forsythe stepped back from the table. Hands that were resting on the edges of the mockup on all four sides disappeared as people retreated into the dark. Remo stayed at the table edge between Chiun and the sniper, drumming his fingers in boredom. He hummed what Forsythe in his terror judged to be "Young at Heart."

The sniper loaded the special bullet into the chamber. It clicked with the deep metal sound of fine tooling. He raised the rifle. Remo yawned.

"Fire," said Chiun.

"I can't miss from here," said the sniper. "I could split an eyelash from here."

"Fire," said Chiun.

"For God's sakes. Not in the basement of the Treasury Building," said Forsythe.

"Well," said the sniper, "whatever Dinko wants, Dinko gets. I think I'm gonna give you another eye."

And as his trigger finger squeezed, Chiun's delicate long-fingernailed hand seemed to flutter under the yellow overhead lights and the DC-10 was no longer in his hands. Only Remo saw it move. But everyone saw it land. Its wings were pressed to the sniper's forehead and the nose and cockpit were embedded in his skull. Blood trickled from the back of the fuselage and as the head went forward, it drowned the tail in the warm red of the sniper's life. The sniper's rifle with the fat barrel clattered onto the mockup, its muzzle resting on the passenger terminal.

Chiun brushed it aside. "A toy," he said.

"No," said Forsythe. "You can't kill someone in the basement of the Treasury Building without a written order."

"Don't let him get away with it," Remo told Forsythe. "Make him clean up the body. He's always leaving bodies around."

"He started it," said Chiun. "If I had started it, I would have cleaned up the body."

"You suckered that numby with the bang-bang into this thing because you were getting bored," said Remo.

"I was merely playing with airplanes," said Chiun. "But everyone knows you whites stick together."

"We have a dead man here," said Forsythe.

"Right. And don't let him get away without cleaning up after himself," said Remo.

"If I were white, you wouldn't say that," said Chiun.

"What are we going to do about the killing?" asked Forsythe.

"Mark it to racial bigotry," said Chiun, who had been hearing these words on his daytime television soap operas and now thought it an appropriate time to use them. "You whites not only smell funny and are stupid but you're also bigots. Racists. And you're not even the best race."

"Don't mind him," said Remo. "He just doesn't want to clean up after himself. Where's the program? And this time, since it's of no value to anyone on earth, it better be the honest one. No fakes."

On the flight to Chicago, Remo examined the box that had words like miniaturization component and input and wondered who would need the assist of creativity that was barely that of a five-year-old. Forsythe had explained that while they needed computers and top scientific minds to approach a substitute creativity, they still hadn't achieved it. They had only a simulation.

After the sniper's death at Chiun's hands. Forsythe had not objected too strongly to leaving snipers behind.

"And your cameramen and sound men and whatever you've got with equipment," Remo had said.

"But this is the most modern technological equipment in existence," Forsythe had protested.

"Did you use it last time?" asked Remo.

"Yes, but . . ."

"It stays here. Along with you."

Forsythe had started to object, but seeing the body of the sniper being lifted to a stretcher and covered with a white sheet had suddenly refocused his thinking.

"At this crucial juncture, we must diversify personnel initiative," he had said.

"That means we make the connection alone," said Remo. "Right?"

"And never come back," predicted Group Leader Forsythe.

Remo saw Chiun motioning.

"And my friend wants to take the model planes."

"Let him have them. My God, do you think we could find someone who would try to stop him?"

Chiun unfolded the half-dozen miniature jets from his kimono as they flew over Lake Erie. Chiun studied the models for a time, then said:

"I do not know how you Westerners do it, but these planes are almost perfect for moving through the air. Without knowledge of the essence of movement or the philosophies I have taught you, these people with just their machines and their typewriters and other foolishnesses have designed these planes. I am amazed."

This too did the Master of Sinanju tell a stewardess who told a pilot who came to where Chiun and Remo sat on the DC-10 headed for Chicago.

"This is a good plane," said Chiun.

"Thank you," said the pilot, in his early fifties, a tanned bright face of an athlete who never stopped caring for himself.

"But it has one flaw," said Chiun and he pointed to the configuration of the tail. "Here it should go in where it goes out."

48

The pilot turned to the stewardess. "You two are kidding me." And then to Chiun, "You're an engineer from McDonnell Douglas, aren't you?"

"What's going on?" asked Remo, who had been napping.

"Well, this gentleman here has just tried to pass himself off as a layman instead of an aeronautics engineer. He just showed me a design I know the company had to reject because they did not have materials that were advanced enough."

"Advanced?" said Chiun and he cackled. "This suggestion I made is thousands of years old."

At O'Hare, a little boy wanted to play with Chiun's model planes. Chiun told him to get his own. They had five hours to wait. It was a little after ten and the contact with Mr. Gordons was set for 3 A.M. in Allegheny's boarding gate Number 8. Forsythe said Gordons had obviously chosen it because of the difficulty of anyone getting to a convenient exit from there. It was, as Forsythe had said, a long box.

Remo and Chiun watched people meet people and people leave. They watched that general small tension that people have while waiting to board. At three, they were resting and should have seen him. That extra sense Reno had about people approaching did not work. Chiun, for the first time in Remo's memory, appeared startled. His eyes opened. Slowly, with the infinitely perfect balance that made him Master of Sinanju, he retreated, putting a ticket booth between himself and Mr. Gordons. Remo remembered Chiun had once said that in extreme emergencies, one could disguise his defenses by hiding his feet.

"Good evening, I'm Mr. Gordons," said the man. Remo judged that they were about even in height, but Gordons was heavier. He moved with an odd slow-

49

ness, not the graceful slowness of Chiun, but rather a deliberate, almost stumbling gliding of the feet forward. When he stopped, the gray suit hardly moved. His lips parted in something that was almost a smile. And stayed that way.

"I'm Remo, your contact. You got the plates?"

"Yes, I do have the plates intended for you. The evening is rather warm, don't you think? I am sorry I do not have a drink to offer you, but we are in an airport terminal and there are no liquor faucets in an airport terminal."

"There aren't any bowling alleys or Mah Jongg tables either. What the hell are you talking about?"

"I am making the greeting that should put you at ease."

"I'm at ease," said Remo. "You got the plates?"

"Yes. I have your package and I can see by your hand that you have mine. I will give you your package for mine," said Mr. Gordons.

"Surrender it, Remo," Chiun called from near the ticket booth. Remo saw a model plane, that perfect missile in the hands of the Master of Sinanju, shoot streaking at Mr. Gordons. With barely a nodding jerk of his head, Mr. Gordons dodged it. And dodged the next. And the next. They cracked the steel and aluminum walls of the boarding corridor, leaving gaping night-filled holes. One took the head off of a wall advertisement for the Pump Room featuring a singer who now had a large bosom and air for a head.

"Remo," yelled Chiun. "Give him what he wants. Give him what he wants."

Remo did not turn around.

"Give me the plates," said Remo.

"Remo. Do not engage in foolishness. Remo."

"I have four plates for fifties and hundreds. The

50

fifties are the Kansas City Federal Reserve Notes 1963 E, front 214, back 108. The hundreds are the Minneapolis Federal Reserve Notes 1974 B, front 118, back 102."

"Who do you work for?" asked Remo, moving his left hand underneath Mr. Gordons's right armpit and pressuring a nerve that would hold and cause pain. The pain was to come on the question and increase during the wait for the answer. That was how it had worked many times before.

"I work for myself. For my existence," said Mr. Gordons.

"Give him what he wants, Remo. Get your arm away," shouted Chiun and then, in the excitement, he gave forth a stream of Korean that sounded to Remo like the phrases he had heard in early training about "things being unworking." In later training, it had always been his training that Chiun said was "unworking." Everything else in the world worked perfectly. But now Remo knew Chiun's shout did not refer to his training.

"Look at the face."

Mr. Gordons was still smiling that silly little smile, so Remo increased the pressure and he felt the skin become rubbery and some sort of bone snap but it was no bone Remo was familiar with.

"Do not do that. You have already caused damage," said Mr. Gordons. "If you continue you will cause a temporary loss of my right side. This could threaten my survival. I must stop you."

Perhaps it was the smile that threw him, the shock of it still being there. Perhaps it was the strange feel of the muscles and flesh. But when Remo went to double the approach with his right hand, using the program as a hard edge instead of his hand, he seemed to slip and his balance was not in balance with Mr. Gordons's and he was going down as Mr. Gordons caught his right elbow and with a steady pressure that he should not have been able to exert from the position he was in, Mr. Gordons closed on Remo's wrist, squeezing to make him release the program.

"Let him have it. Give it up," yelled Chiun.

"Give it up, hell," said Remo and whipped up a knee to take out Mr. Gordons's groin. But the knee flailed in the air as Remo's right shoulder felt hot irons ripping at the tendons.

Remo saw the flash of Chiun's kimono come at him and then, to his shock, he did not see the awesome skill of the frail hands tear the smile from Mr. Gordons's face. Instead, he saw Chiun come at his own hands. Remo felt Chiun's long nails pry open his right hand. And then the program was gone. Mr. Gordons had it, dropping the plates as he pushed the program into his shirt.

"Thank you," said Mr. Gordons, who then walked evenly away despite his damaged right side. Remo spun back to his feet and, at an angle to compensate for the damage to his arm, took the first step toward catching that sandy blond head and dismembering its supporting neck. But Chiun's foot was faster, and Remo tripped tumbling forward, groaning in pain from his shoulder. Chiun circled and stood between Remo and Mr. Gordons who was disappearing from the boarding area into the main lobby.

"What'd you do that for? I had him. I had him," yelled Remo, his eyes tearing in frustration.

"We must flee and I must bind your wounds, foolish one," said Chiun.

"You let him get the program. You let him get it. Now we'll never see him again."

52

"Let us hope for that," said Chiun and with his long delicate fingers began probing the shoulder muscles of his young student. With strips from his own kimono, he bound the arm so there would be no more tearing and then took him to a ticket counter where the Master of Sinanju asked where there was sun and sea water. And being told many places, he selected the nearest, St. Thomas in the Virgin Islands, which was unknown to the Master of Sinanju but which he decided had probably been discovered only recently, in the last five hundred years or so.

With the plates for the white man's paper money, Chiun made a package. And with the other paper printings, their stamps, pasted on the price of their mailing. And with their pens that needed no dipping into ink, not even brushes were these pens, he prepared a missive for Smith whose empire had employed this latest Master of Sinanju.

Dear Harold Smith, Mr.

Lo, these many years has the House of Sinanju served your empire and lo, these many years has your graciousness been bestowed upon our little village. Our children and our poor and our aged eat and are clothed and sleep under roofs that are of new materials.

Never has the empire of Smith been negligent of its obligations. Full well has it paid its gold at appointed times. Without these obligations being met, the village of Sinanju would starve for the soil is rocky and the sea does not yield fish from the cold bay. The services of the Master of Sinanju for centuries has enabled our people to first, eat, and then

53

to live in dignity. You have met your agreement made more than a decade ago.

The Master of Sinanju has also met his. The Master was contracted to take a normal white man and to teach him Sinanju. As much, you remember it was stipulated, as was needed so that he need not carry weapons to perform. This the young man learned. Within the very first year, he learned this. But he has learned much more than your gold purchased. He was given more than your gold could buy. He has become Sinanju more than anyone, even Japanese and other Koreans, outside of Sinanju has ever become.

He has taken the sun source to his heart and this you did not pay for. He has conquered his body and become its master and this you did not pay for. He has joined and been given Sinanju in the completeness of what he could grasp. This you did not pay for and this the House of Sinanju would never sell. For Sinanju is not for sale; only its services are.

Therefore, with much regret and with gratitude, the Master must inform you that Sinanju terminates the agreement. We will find sustenance elsewhere for the village, as will Remo and I.

Incidentally, Remo being not only white but American white, will naturally have special affection for his homeland and should at a later time you need his services, you would be highly considered by him.

Enclosed are the pieces of metal you wished. The mission is over. The contract is over.

Chiun made the mark of Sinanju, an inverted trapezoid with a vertical line bisecting it—a figure for house—and then one for "absolute" which was more complicated but which represented his name and title, and with the envelope he had purchased along with the stamps and wrapping paper and stationery and pen at the airport merchant's, he covered the missive and made sure it was placed into the metal boxes which were emptied regularly and delivered by messengers. Not since Genghis Khan had there been such a service so well protected. Not a mean accomplishment, for Westerners.

When he returned to the bench where Remo waited, he was pleased to see Remo sitting with his weight properly adjusted for his other muscles to support the torn ones. Often this young man's creative and learned knowledge had pleased the master to gladness. But one could not acknowledge such gladness for the young man's arrogance was already too much to bear.

"What were you doing, Little Father, writing a book? You almost filled a whole pad," said Remo.

"I was telling Emperor Smith of your misfortunes, of your damage."

"Why? I'll be okay."

Chiun shook his head with exaggerated solemnity.

"Yes. I know that and you know that, but emperors are emperors, even if you wish to call them directors or presidents or whatever you wish to call them. And when an assassin is wounded, no matter how highly prized he is, emperors have no use for them."

"Smitty?"

"Yes. It is sad, my son. A wounded assassin has no home. Emperors' loyalties have limits."

"But I'm part of the organization. I'm the only one outside of Smitty who knows what we do."

"It is a sad lesson of growing up you are learning," said Chiun. "But do not fear. If emperors have no loyalty for assassins, yet there is always a market for our services. In the peace of Rome there was need, in

55

the order of the Khan's sons there was need, and in the turmoil years, there is most definitely a need. Worry not. Rome is gone, the Chinese dynasties are gone. Sinanju lives."

"I can't believe Smitty would feel that way," said Remo, and Chiun quieted him, for the young man needed rest for now. Their airplane would be leaving soon and this flight business, while it appeared to do little harm, did upset the blood in people as did the changing of the moons. But white men did not know this. Even few yellow men did.

When they boarded the plane for St. Thomas, due to arrive at the airport named after a dead emperor, Truman, in less than five hours, Chiun noticed a small metallic spur implanted in Remo's clothes. And since he did not know what it was, he did not throw it away. It might be that of Mr. Gordons, whose technique in all the centuries of Sinanju was unknown, and who Remo foolishly had chosen to defy. But this could be forgiven Remo. He was young, not even yet sixty in years.

Remo did not know that to confront the unknown, one must first stand aside and watch it and wait until it was known. Remo did not know that the Master of Sinanju hoped that Mr. Gordons would continue his adventures and by so doing become known in his methods as had the Hashashins of Arabia with their methods of fanaticism and skill.

Another Master had encountered the Hashashins when they were a new thing and he immediately terminated services with Islamabad, and waited and watched and worked elsewhere as year by year the Hashashins became more known in their methods. So good were they, the very name assassin came from them. And that Master passed on to the following

Master what he knew. And the following Master passed on what he knew, as each generation watched and avoided the rich markets of Araby. It was eighty years before Sinanju realized how the Hashashins used hashish on followers and how they recruited an outer layer of fanatics willing to die for paradise, and these fanatics protected their inner layer of leaders.

When this was known, the House of Sinanju returned to the wealthy of the Islamic world, and, in one night, followed a drugged warrior of the house of Hashashins and waited until the first signs of their smoke appeared and then slaughtered them in their caves to the very last man. The Hashashins were no more.

So too with Mr. Gordons. If not this year, then next. And if not the next, then surely the year after that. But some year, either Chiun or Remo or Remo's followers would make Mr. Gordons's methods known. And then the House of Sinanju would return to the wealth of America.

But not now. Now was a time to run. Let Mr. Gordons have his decade or generation or century. There were other markets for Sinanju.

Chiun made note of where the metal spur had been placed, saw it had not punctured Remo's skin, and put it in his own kimono for keeping and examination. It might have come from Mr. Gordons. In that case it was worth examining.

As the plane powered into the sky, the package Chiun had addressed was picked up by the U.S. Postal Service. It was headed toward a sanitarium in Rye, New York, called Folcroft.

There any one of hundreds of electronic technicians could have told the Master of Sinanju that if he wanted to escape from the man who gave him that metal spur, he should have given it to the first passing stranger.

Provided the stranger was going to another part of the world.

CHAPTER FOUR

Morris "Moe" Alstein owned the only bar on Chicago's South Side that lost money. He had bought it in the 1960s when it was a dowdy neighborhood tavern that regularly gave its owner a healthy $40,000 a year off the top and another $40,000 to $50,000 from non-taxable ancillary rights like numbers and loansharking and bookmaking.

Moe Alstein's renovators tore out the rotting wood molding, swept away the sawdust on the floor and installed an elegant mahogany bar, hidden lighting, new bathrooms, fine tables, new walls, a new inlaid floor, broke down walls to give his customers more space, built a stage and with the aid of a talent scout and a hot new young emcee, Alstein managed to turn around the financial picture to an initial loss of $247,000 the first year and $40,000 each ensuing year. Some attributed this loss to a change of market direction—that is, he lost the regular customers and did not replace them with others. That is what people said publicly.

Privately, they might tell very close friends with

tight mouths that Moe's habits might have something to do with his losses. Moe liked pistols, and in the basement of the Eldorado Spa, changed from Murray's, he had a pistol range. He would practice there daily. The trouble started when he moved the basement range to the stage. He made it part of the floorshow. To show how good he was, he shot earrings off customers and glasses out of hands. But customer loyalty was fickle in Chicago's South Side. Even though Moe "never fucking hit anyone," the clientele dwindled.

Fortunately, Moe had an alternate profession that compensated for the bar's losses. Which was what Mr. Gordons wished to speak to him about that morning.

"I don't know you," said Moe to the gently-smiling man with the neatly combed sandy-blond hair and the right arm that moved properly but seemed slightly lower than his left.

"My name is Mr. Gordons and I'm sorry I cannot offer you a drink but this is your establishment and it is incumbent upon you to offer me a drink."

"All right, whaddya want?"

"Nothing, thank you, I do not drink. I wish you to attempt to kill someone with your pistol."

"Hey, whaddya, out of your head?" said Moe Alstein. Moe was slight and shorter than this man. His eyes were sharp blue and his face pinched like a stretched cellophane bag. His eyes did not trust the bland features of this man but even if they had, he wasn't going to do contract work for someone who came in off the street.

"I do not understand your colloquialism, 'out of your head,'" said Mr. Gordons.

"First off, I don't kill people. Second off, if I did,

I wouldn't do it for some bimbo who comes in off the street, and third off, who the fuck are you?"

"I am not sure that your expressions are accurate. That is, I think you are saying things for your protection and not because they are true. This I have found to be commonplace, so do not take offense as people often do when they are exposed in inaccuracies. I have something you want."

"What I want is you should get out of here while you can still walk," said Alstein.

"Not necessarily," said Mr. Gordons and from his jacket pocket, he took a fresh stack of fifty $100 bills. He placed it on the table between them. Then he put a second package on top of the first package. And a third and a fourth. And a fifth. Moe wondered how the man kept his suit so neat with all that money stashed in the pockets. When the pile was ten stacks high, Mr. Gordons started a second pile. And when that was ten high, he stopped.

"That's a hundred grand," said Moe Alstein. "A real hundred grand. No government frame ever offered a hundred grand."

"I assumed you would think that."

"No hit ever paid a hundred grand. I mean, not a regular contract, sort of," said Allstein.

"And these bills are valid," said Mr. Gordons. "Examine the silk fiber, the engraving around the face of Franklin, the clarity of the serial numbers which are sequential and not all the same."

"Real," said Moe Alstein. "But you know, I can't move right away. To take off a capo is a tough thing. I got to spread some of this around."

"This is not for your usual work of helping an ethnic group settle disputes among members of their crime families. This is for a simple hitting."

61

"Hit," said Moe.

"Hit. Thank you. It is now hit," said Mr. Gordons. "This hit is simple. I will personally show you where he is."

Moe Alstein's head jerked back in shock.

"Whaddya paying me for, if you're gonna be there? I mean, the point of getting someone else to make the hit is that you're not there. Unless you want to watch the guy suffer?"

"No. I hope to watch you kill him. There are two people. They are very interesting. Especially an elderly yellow man who is most interesting. Every movement of his is most natural and seen in people, yet it accomplishes much more than other people's movements. Him I wish to see. But I cannot observe properly if I must also perform."

"Oh, two hits," said Alstein. "It'll cost you more."

"I will provide you more."

Alstein shrugged. "It's your money."

"It's your money," said Mr. Gordons and pushed the two piles of bills across the table.

"When do you want these guys hit?"

"Soon. First I must get the others."

"Others?"

"There will be others with us. I must get them."

"Wait a minute," said Moe, backing away from the table. "I don't mind you watching. You're as guilty as me before a court, probably more so. I'm just doing a contract. You'd, for sure, do life, know what I mean? I got something over you. But strangers, witnesses, they got something over me. And you. Know what I mean?"

"Yes, I understand," said Mr. Gordons. "But they will not be only witnesses. I am hiring them too."

"I don't need help. Really. I'm good," said Alstein

and told the bartender to get up on the stage with a glass.

The bartender, a balding black man who had become very good at the Chicago *Tribune*'s crossword puzzle, rarely having anyone but Alstein to serve, looked up from his paper and winced.

"Make it two glasses," called Alstein.

"I quit," said the black man.

Moe Alstein's right hand went into his jacket and came out with a whizbang of a .357 Magnum, chrome plated like a big shiny cannon. It went bang like a roof coming off. The heavy bullet blasted a shelf of glasses and shattered a mirror above the bartender's head. Shards scattered over the inlaid floor like shiny pieces of sharp-edged dew under a morning sun.

The bartender went under the bar. A black hand with a long champagne glass at the very end of its fingertips came up over the bar.

Boom went the .357 Magnum. Splat went the plywood backing where the mirror had been. The hand now held only a champagne stem.

"See, I don't need no help," said Moe Alstein, and raising his voice, he yelled, "you can come out now, Willie."

"I'm not Willie," said the voice, still beneath the bar. "Willie quit."

"When?" asked Alstein, his eyes squinting, personal hurt all over his face.

"When you had to order the last mirror. The one that's on the floor now."

"Why'd he quit?"

"Some people don't like to be shot at, Mr. Alstein."

"I never hit anybody I didn't plan to. Never fucking hit anybody. You anti-Semites are all alike," said Moe Alstein, and confided to Mr. Gordons that

63

it was the same virulent anti-Semitism that had ruined his bar business.

"People might feel endangered even though you did not physically hurt them," suggested Mr. Gordons.

"Bullshit," said Moe Alstein. "An anti-Semite is an anti-Semite. You Jewish? You don't look Jewish."

"No," said Mr. Gordons.

"You look WASP."

"WASP?"

"White Anglo-Saxon Protestant."

"No."

"Polish?"

"No."

"German?"

"No."

"Greek?"

"No."

"What are you?" asked Alstein.

"A human being."

"I know that. What kind?"

"Creative," said Mr. Gordons with what sounded like pride.

"Some of my best friends are creatives," said Moe Alstein and wondered if creatives had a history of anti-Semitism and how someone who spoke English without an accent and seemed so knowledgeable didn't know the term "WASP."

But as he left, Mr. Gordons knew the term and would never forget it, filing it under the ethnic divisions whereby American people told themselves apart, sometimes for purposes of social intercourse, and sometimes not. It was a high variable without any real constant, decided Mr. Gordons.

The next person to see him that day was a United States Marine sergeant at a recruiting booth in downtown Chicago. Mr. Gordons had many questions for the sergeant in Marine dress blue with shirt and ribbons and a face that gleamed with the red puffiness of too many whiskeys and beers.

"Do you know how to use a flamethrower?" asked Mr. Gordons.

"And you will too if you're a Marine. How old are you?"

"What do you mean by that?" asked Mr. Gordons.

"When were you born?"

"Oh, I see what you mean. I guess I don't look one year old."

"You look twenty-nine. You're twenty-nine, right. That's a good age," said the sergeant who had a quota to fill and could not fill it with people who were forty years old.

"Yes, twenty-nine," said Mr. Gordons, and the sergeant, thinking this recruit might be a little light on the intelligence, insisted he take the standard mental test before the sergeant went any further.

What happened left the sergeant shaken and wide-eyed, which might have accounted for his susceptibility to the offer that ensued.

The sergeant saw the recruit fill in the question forms, click, click, click click, without a pause, without apparently even reading the questions while he continued to ask the sergeant about skills with flame-throwers. If that wasn't bad enough, when the sergeant looked at the answers, all were correct but for one requiring identification of some common tools. It was the highest score the sergeant had ever seen. No one had ever filled out the test that accurately and that quickly before.

"You only missed one," said the sergeant.

"Yes. I do not recognize those tools. I have never seen them before."

"Well, this one here is a common grease gun."

"Yes. Because of the very high tolerance of many machines like cars here on earth, grease would be used to make metal parts, let us say, slide without friction. The grease is anti-friction, correct," said Mr. Gordons.

"Yeah," said the sergeant. "You know everything but what a grease gun was."

"Yes. But I am more secure knowing that I could have figured out what a grease gun might be used for. I could not have done that just a week ago. But I can now. Have you ever thought of becoming wealthy and leaving the Pitulski Marines?" said Mr. Gordons.

"Pitulski's my name," said Sergeant Pitulski. "You're looking at my name. That's not my unit," he said, tapping the black plastic rectangle with white lettering that he wore over his right shirt pocket.

"Ah, yes. The name. Well, not everything is perfect. Would you like to be wealthy?" said Mr. Gordons, and before Sergeant Pitulski could gather his wits, he was agreeing to meet Mr. Gordons the next night at the Eldorado Spa owned by Moe Alstein and he was sure he could bring a flamethrower with him. Guaranteed. In fact he wished he had the flamethrower now so he could protect the "you-know-what" Mr. Gordons had just given him in two stacks and which Sergeant Pitulski had quickly shoved into his top desk drawer which he locked. In his stunned daze, he had only one sort of well, silly, question: Why did Mr. Gordons apologize for not offering a drink when he entered?

"Isn't that what you're supposed to do upon meeting?"

"No. Not necessarily," said Sergeant Pitulski.

"When is it appropriate?"

"When someone comes to your home or office if your office is allowed to serve alcohol."

"I see. What do you ordinarily say?"

" 'Hello' is all right," said Sergeant Pitulski.

One hour and seven minutes later, Mr. Gordons entered a sports store near Chicago's Loop. Black rubber suits and yellow air tanks hung on the walls. Underwater spear guns were racked behind the counter. A glass case was filled with diving masks.

"Can I help you?" said the salesman.

"Hello is all right," said Mr. Gordons, and twenty minutes later the salesman took the one opportunity of his life to be rich. In fact, when he told the store-owner that the owner was a "stupid sonuvabitch who didn't know sales from his rectum," he was already a rich man. Before he showed up the next night at the Eldorado Spa on Chicago's South Side, he had deposited his riches in ten separate banks under ten different names, because he thought a hundred-thousand-dollar cash deposit might raise some questions.

His name was Robert Jellicoe and when he walked into the Eldorado the next night, he was staggering under his load of tanks and rubber suits and three spear guns. He had been unable to make up his mind as to which gun to take. He had only shot fish before. So he decided to take all three.

Mr. Gordons and two other men sat around a table. The only other sound in the empty bar was the light hum of an air conditioner. Jellicoe wondered why someone would spend so much money on furnishing the spa, as someone obviously had, and then use a long section of plywood across the whole back of the bar. Particularly when a mirror would have fit just perfectly.

"I got a question," said Sergeant Pitulski, wearing a green suit, white shirt, and blue tie. "How we gonna get this past customs at the airport?" He patted the khaki-colored double tanks of his flamethrower.

"And my gun," said Moe Alstein, patting his shoulder holster.

"My diving gear won't have any trouble," said Jellicoe. "Lots of people bring skin-diving gear on vacations. I have. Many times."

"You are bringing none of your equipment," said Mr. Gordons. "In its present form."

"I gotta have my special gun," said Alstein.

"My gear is broken in," said Jellicoe. "I can't use new gear."

"I can get along with any old shit," said Sergeant Pitulski. "I'm a Marine. The worse the equipment, the better I use it."

Mr. Gordons quieted all. He bade them wait outside. Alstein said he should stay because it was his place. Mr. Gordons took Alstein by the neck, turned him upside down, moved him easily to the door, righted the flailing man on his feet, then motioned for the others to follow. They did. He locked the door and thirty minutes later returned with a package for each.

The largest went to Jellicoe. It was the size and shape of a large suitcase, but it weighed almost as much as a trunk. In fact, it weighed just as much as his tanks and wet suit and spear guns had. The next largest went to Sergeant Pitulski. His was almost as large, very heavy, and something sloshed around inside. Alstein got the smallest, a box fit for a necklace.

At O'Hare, boarding for St. Thomas, when customs opened all packages, Jellicoe saw in his a metallic engraving with a small yellow sun in a corner as if someone had melted the yellow from the covering of his tanks. Around the engraving was a black rubber frame, and Jellicoe, who had failed in the second year of engineering at college, recognized the materials of his scuba gear. But in different form.

It was not possible, but that was what it was. He knew. He knew that somehow Mr. Gordons had been able to condense the materials and compress them into that small engraving. Jellicoe felt his stomach flutter and then his knees become weak. There was that silly smile on Gordons's face, and Jellicoe said he was all right. He waited by the doorway that scanned boarders for metal, watched Alstein's surprise when he realized he was carrying a perfect likeness of the statue of Abraham Lincoln—in chrome—and Pitulski stared dully ahead when the customs inspector opened a large steel bust of George Washington and five steel vials of liquid.

"What's in these bottles?" asked an inspector.

"No flammable liquids," said Mr. Gordons, moving to the customs table. "More importantly, pressure drops will not affect them in the air."

"Yeah, but what are they?"

When Jellicoe heard the answer—the basic elements that went into the flammable liquid of a flame-thrower—he swallowed hard. He rested his arm on an adjacent knee-high ashtray, steadied himself, told Mr. Gordons he was ill, and was allowed to go out through the doorway metal scanner by both Mr. Gordons and the customs people.

He moved, feet shuffling like a sick man, until he was out of sight of the boarding gate, and then ran. His feet were weak, but his lungs could go a mile, he thought, just to run and breathe, run past the incredible fear that had filled him, the horror of who he had agreed to do murder for. He did not know who the man was but he knew this man was beyond any in skill he had ever heard of. And if this man, Mr. Gordons, needed help in carrying off a killing, well then, God help them all.

At the Braniff counter, he cut toward a stationery stand, then ducked into a dark bar, ordered a drink, went into the bathroom, into a john with a door, stood on the toilet seat, crunched down his body, and waited. He glanced at his watch. It was twenty minutes to flight time. It was a good thing, he thought, that all flights going near Cuba were checked for possible hijacker weapons. It was a good thing he had had a chance to see what he was dealing with.

With only ten minutes left there came a knock on the toilet door. Which was strange because no one could see his feet resting on the toilet seat.

"Robert Jellicoe. Come out. You will miss your plane."

It was Mr. Gordons's voice.

CHAPTER FIVE

The Caribbean sun is hot and its waters aquamarine. Its islands are rock clusters rising from the sea where men scramble for a living on the poor soil and where long brown furry mongooses scurry in the underbrush, the descendants of the rodents imported from India to rid the islands of green snakes. There are no more green snakes but the mongoose has become a problem.

Chiun, the Master of Sinanju, thought on this and on other things he had heard.

"These are islands of survivors," he said. "The sun is good for your shoulder. The salt water is good for the air you breathe. It is a good place to heal."

"I don't know, Little Father," said Remo. He reclined on the porch of the house they had rented overlooking Magen's Bay, a wood and glass house with three porches and a living room that extended out over a ledge, so one felt he could look anywhere and be surrounded by the sea below. Water dripped from Remo's swimming trunks, the result of a four-mile swim, two out and two back, taken under Chiun's watchful eye. It had been that way every day and when Remo had protested that his shoulder needed rest to heal, not exercise, Chiun had sneered and said, "Like your fraction back, I suppose."

"Like my what?"

"Like your fraction back. Every year he hurts his knees and they give him a year's rest, and then he comes back and hurts his knees even worse."

"Who are you talking about?" said Remo. "And if you can't answer that, what are you talking about will do."

"The fraction back on your television games. You know, where all those fat men knock each other down and jump on each other."

"Football?"

"Correct. Football. And the fraction back. The funny looking one, who talks funny and wears ladies' stockings in the selling moments on television."

Remo nodded. "He's a quarterback."

Chiun nodded. "Correct. A fraction back. Anyway, we do not want your shoulder like his knees. So you exercise."

And that was that, and now Reno lounged in a chair, dripping, and heard Chiun say that this island of survivors was a good place to heal.

"I don't know," said Remo. "I get the feeling I don't belong here. It's like I'm not attuned to it. Shouldn't I, for healing, return to where I was born?"

Chiun slowly shook his head, his wispy beard caught by a southwest breeze blowing in across islands they could not see.

"No. On these islands, only the invaders survive, like the mongoose. Where are the Caribbe Indians, you should ask yourself."

"I don't know. Drunk in Charlotte Amalie," said

72

Remo, referring to the shopping district of St. Thomas where liquor, because of the tax-free status, was almost as cheap as soda. Every other store in this duty-free port seemed to sell Seiko watches which were also a major attraction for cruise passengers who left their money there along with the paleness of their skins.

"The Caribbe Indians who lived here are no more," said Chiun. "They lived full and happy lives here until the Spanish came and so cruel were the new overlords that all the Caribbe Indians climbed to a cliff and threw themselves off. But before they died, their chief promised the gods would avenge them."

"And did they?"

"According to the story that is told widely here, yes. An earthquake destroyed a city, killing thousands, thirty thousands."

"But not all the Spaniards," said Remo.

"No. Because he who leaves vengeance to others will never slake his thirst. But Sinanju, as you know, is not vengeance. Vengeance is a foolish thing. Our art of Sinanju is life. To live is what we are. Our very services of death are purposed in the survival of the village. That is what makes us powerful. He who lives is strong. Look verily at the many black faces on these islands, brought in chains they were. Whipped they were. Set here on these barren lands to harvest sugar for others. But who survived? The proud Caribbe Indians seeking vengeance by their gods, or the blacks who day by day bore their children, built their homes, and tethered their anger? The black lives. The mongoose lives. The green snake and the Caribbe Indians are no more."

"What sort of pride did the green snake have?"

"It is a story that you should not be thinking about vengeance with Mr. Gordons. It is a story that you

73

should follow the lessons of survival which is Sinanju's training. It is not a story about green snakes."

"Sounded like green snakes to me," said Remo, knowing this would rile Chiun, and he was not disappointed for he heard snatches of Korean which amounted to the inability of transforming a pale piece of pig's ear into silk, or mud into diamonds. It would, Remo knew, become an evening lecture on how thousands of years of Sinanju had come down to a waste with a white man. But Remo would not pay attention to those words. For what Chiun had said by his actions had been spoken loud and clear.

The aged Korean had left his belongings in the States: his robes and, more importantly, his special television setup provided by upstairs on which Chiun could watch his daytime soap operas without missing the ones that ran concurrently. The device taped the other channels so Chiun would have hours of uninterrupted soap opera. Chiun had also left his autographed picture of Rad Rex, star of *As the Planet Revolves,* who at this very moment, Chiun had noted, was pondering whether or not to tell Mrs. Loretta Lamont that her daughter's abortion had disclosed a cancerous tumor that somehow would prove Wyatt Walton was innocent of leaving his wife and seven children in Majorca before he came to Mrs. Lamont's house as a spiritual adviser. Chiun was missing this, he noted.

And if Chiun could leave his daytime dramas, certainly Remo without second thought could leave the organization. But on this point Chiun had not dwelled too long. Survival was what he had daily lectured to Remo since they had come to St. Thomas almost a week before. But it was leaving the organization that bothered Remo to his very essence.

On the other end of the island at the Harry Truman

74

Airport, an American Airlines jet was landing with another person who was bothered to his very essence. But unlike Remo, Robert Jellicoe showed it. While all the other passengers went to the front of the airplane, Robert Jellicoe went to the rear into the little lavatory and upchucked again. He did not bother to lock the door or even stay and hide, but flushed, left, and stumbled back down the aisle of the plane and down the debarking ramp into the terminal where Mr. Gordons, Moe Alstein, and Sergeant Pitulski were waiting. Alstein noted that the mugginess made his suit feel like liver. Sergeant Pitulski said the only cure for that was a shot of Seagrams Seven and a bottle of Bud.

Mr. Gordons forbade drinking. In the Windward Hotel overlooking the port, Mr. Gordons asked all three to wait for him a few moments. There was some shopping he had to do. Sergeant Pitulski told Mr. Gordons to take his time and when he was gone, ordered a bottle of Seagrams and a case of beer and proceeded to go shot and quaff until he confessed that today's Marines weren't really Marines. The real Marines didn't fight in Vietnam, otherwise America wouldn't have had to pull out, leaving unfinished business. The real Marines were those who served at San Diego, Japan, Cherry Point, North Carolina, and Parris Island.

"You serve at those places?" asked Moe Alstein.

As a matter of fact, Sergeant Pitulski had, Sergeant Pitulski admitted.

"Thought so," said Alstein.

Jellicoe was quiet. Alstein offered him a drink. Jellicoe refused. Alstein asked what the matter was.

"Nothing," said Jellicoe.

"You know, I don't like working with you either,

you anti-Semitic sonuvabitch," said Alstein. "You're
an amateur. Amateurs. I could get killed with amateurs."

"Could?" said Jellicoe.

"Whaddya mean amateurs? I'm a Marine."

"You're a rummy," said Alstein.

"You don't know what Marines can do," said Pitulski.

"Get drunk and lose fistfights," said Alstein. "Jeez,
I wish I had my weapon with me. I wish I had it."

"You will," said Jellicoe.

"Naah," said Alstein. "He took it in Chicago. That
Gordons is a funny guy. I bet he brings me some
cheap piece of shit that I have to stick in the hit's
nostrils to get a piece of the nose. You'll see. Everybody laughs at the chrome plate and the size of a .357
Magnum, the chrome being my own idea. But with
that little doozy, I'm king."

"You'll get your gun back," said Jellicoe.

"Bullshit. He couldn't get a gun through customs.
I know. They're spooky about those flights that go
past Cuba."

"Marines could get guns into Cuba," said Pitulski.
"As a matter of fact we got them there. Gitmo. God
bless the United States Marines," he sobbed and
moaned that he had deserted the only family he ever
had, the Marines, and for what? Money. Filthy, dirty
rotten money. Even stole a flamethrower—which the
Marines would miss. Not like the Air Force where you
could lose a fleet of planes and the government would
resupply five squadrons. The Marines treasured their
weapons.

"Shut up," said Alstein. "You're worried about a
dinky six-hundred-a-month job and I've got a whole
career riding on this."

"You'll both get your weapons," said Jellicoe.

"Not the same one," said Alstein. "Not the same feel."

"The exact feel," said Jellicoe.

"Not the same serial numbers."

"The same serial numbers. Right down to the pits in the chrome," said Jellicoe.

When Mr. Gordons returned to the hotel suite, he carried valises, swinging them slowly and easily. He instructed everyone to bring the packages he had given them back in Chicago and which had passed inspection at the airport, into his room. When he saw Pitulski stumble drunkenly, he put the bags down lightly.

"Negative. Cease. Not that much drink. Over-abundance. Cease. Cease," said Mr. Gordons, and twice smacked the reddish face of Sergeant Pitulski, making the crimson cheeks shine just a little more brightly. He upended him and walked him to a closet where he locked the door on the upside-down Marine.

"Excessive drinking is dangerous, especially when people have tools in their hands and are responsible for the survival of other things," said Mr. Gordons.

"He didn't have any tools," said Alstein.

"I'm talking about his skills as tools and my survival," said Mr. Gordons. He nodded to the bags and Jellicoe bent down, gripped a handle, and jerked—himself to the carpeted hotel room floor. The valise wouldn't move.

"That is a bit excessive for you, isn't it?" said Gordons. "I will take them," and, as if the valises were filled with woven wicker and handkerchiefs, Mr. Gordons lifted them and walked them smoothly into the other room.

"You're pretty weak there, Jellicoe," said Alstein.

About a half-hour later, as Alstein read a magazine in the suite's living room and Jellicoe stared dumbly at the door that Mr. Gordons had locked behind himself, the door suddenly opened.

"What's that?" asked Mr. Gordons.

"Nothing," said Alstein.

"I hear something."

Alstein and Jellicoe shrugged.

"I hear something. I know I hear something," said Mr. Gordons. A canvas cloth covered his hands, at least where his hands should be, but the vague outline under the canvas was that of tools attached to his wrists. "Open that closet."

When Alstein opened the closet door, they all saw Sergeant Pitulski, upside down and red-faced. Alstein lowered an ear.

"He's humming 'The Halls of Montezuma,' " said Alstein.

"Right side him up," said Mr. Gordons. "And for him, no drinks. You others seem capable of drinking without wanting to become disorderly, so you may drink. But not Pitulski."

"How we gonna keep him from drinking if we drink?" asked Alstein.

"You mean just because a person sees someone else drink, he wants to drink?"

"It works that way," said Alstein.

"Feed that in," said Jellicoe.

"I just have," said Gordons.

"As a seventy-three percent positive," said Jellicoe.

"How are you using that?" asked Mr. Gordons.

"As in seventy-three percent of the time that would be accurate."

"Done, but with the standard deviation for human inaccuracy," said Mr. Gordons and disappeared into his room. When he returned, he held in his two hands —they appeared normal now to Jellicoe, as he had expected they would—a .357 Magnum with the bullets clutched in his palm, and the spear guns. The flamethrower was strung around his left arm; the scuba tanks and rubber suit hung from his right. The flamethrower sloshed. It was filled.

He gave Alstein the gun, Jellicoe the underwater gear, and put the flamethrower down at Pitulski's feet. Pitulski was snoozing in an armchair.

Alstein looked at the shiny chrome. He bounced the gun flat on his palm. He spun the cylinder. He looked at the cartridges and with his fingers isolated one and held it up to the light.

"Same gun, same bullets," said Alstein. "I know this cartridge. Two days ago I was loading and I became fascinated by the bronze case. I always am. Bullets are beautiful. Art. Really beautiful. And with a pin, for the hell of it, I scratched my initials in it. Not deep. I don't want to weaken the shell. But here it is."

"I was wondering about that," said Mr. Gordons. "I thought perhaps you had some special system. But I see you are about to put it into a different chamber."

"The chambers are all the same," said Alstein.

"They are not. Neither are the bullets. They are all different in size and shape but you cannot perceive that. Here. Let me load the same way you had them loaded."

Alstein watched and commented that he couldn't see how Mr. Gordons could tell. But that wasn't the first crazy thing and it wasn't the last. It was not only the first time Alstein had gone on a team hit, but also the first time that he was wired and given what Mr. Gordons called a tracker. He made Alstein stand in

79

the center of the room and turn around slowly. When the buttonlike thing taped to Alstein's stomach vibrated, Mr. Gordons said the two targets were in the direction Alstein was facing.

"You mean, here in the room?"

Mr. Gordons laid out a map of St. Thomas. "No. Roughly either the Peterborg Estates or over Magen's Bay. When you're pointed toward them, you'll feel the vibrations. They will get stronger as you get closer."

Sergeant Pitulski yawned and blinked his eyes and attempted to focus his mind. Something was caught in the back of his shirt.

He reached behind him and with great effort tore it out from his shirt. It was a little metal spur with spikes. He pressed it in his fingers and then, to test its hardness, bit into it.

Alstein spun around and grabbed his stomach.

"It's burning, it's burning, it's burning," he cried.

"Turn away from Pitulski," said Gordons and with his fingers snapped the spur from Pitulski's mouth as if preventing a dog from chewing on some unclean thing.

Jellicoe watched Mr. Gordons's fingers reshape the spur and Alstein sighed with relief. So that was how Mr. Gordons found him in the bathroom of the O'Hare Airport, thought Jellicoe. The spurs were miniature transmitters—homing devices—and when Sergeant Pitulski had bitten into his, he somehow had changed the frequency to that of the two targets. Jellicoe felt around his back and his fingers closed on a beautiful sharp spur. He moved his hand away quickly. Apparently Mr. Gordons had not seen him. He would leave it there until he saw a chance of escape. And this time he would not carry his own beacon. He would throw it away and flee. When he had a chance.

"Buncha nuts," mumbled Alstein and then took a fast look at the photographs of the two hits. One, according to Mr. Gordons, was called "high probability Remo" and the other "high probability Chiun." The Oriental was Chiun. Mr. Gordons believed this because that is what he heard them call each other.

The photos looked as if someone had shot them head high but when Jellicoe picked up the two sheets of paper, black and gray ink came off on his right thumb in a smear like a small Greek shield. It shone glossy. They were not photographs. They were incredibly fine etchings. Done with ink.

Who was this Mr. Gordons? What were his powers and where did he get them? He was like a walking laboratory and manufacturing plant, all in one. Jellicoe shuddered and tried to think of more pleasant times.

"I'll be back in an hour with the job done and we can all go home," said Alstein. But he was not back in an hour. He didn't even find the house until sunrise. The vibrating button worked fine, but it seemed to vibrate right over fields or directly up rocky inclines and it was dawn before Alstein had worked out the correct combination of roads for his car and stood before a little wooden house with an excellent view of a wide jade-blue bay and the waters below. A long furry rat-like creature scurried under a banana palm. A small brown lizard clinging to the side of the house looked balefully behind his head with eyes that rotated.

Moe Alstein cocked his gun, knocked with his left hand on the door. No one answered. He knocked again.

81

"Who is it?" came a voice.

"Western Union," said Alstein. "I got a message for you."

"Who for?"

"A Remo something."

"Just a minute."

Alstein raised the gun and aimed just above the doorknob. When the knob turned and the door opened slightly he let go with the first shot that took off a fist-sized hunk from the edge of the wooden door. The door slammed open and Alstein moved in, looking for the wounded body. But there were only splinters and a big hole through the sliding glass door at the other end of the house. There wasn't even any blood. A bearded old gook stuck his head out of a door. Alstein squeezed off a shot at the bearded face. But no blood. No body smacked back as if hit by a sledge-hammer. Just a big scoop out of the wall.

Where was the person who had opened the door? Where? Moe Alstein stepped back in sudden panic. He would retreat to the road and blast them from there. There was nothing in this house that could stop a .357 Magnum.

But what had happened? He had to have hit some-one but there was no blood. And he had had the little gook perfect. He could take the bowl off a champagne glass at thirty feet; he wasn't going to miss a whole head. The door behind him had to have sent wood splinters into someone. You don't open a door without a hand. As Alstein stepped back, he felt a little sting-ing in his gun hand. He saw an arm over his shoulder coming directly down to his right wrist. There was a guy on the ledge above the door, resting on it as if it were a wide hammock.

"Hi. I'm Remo. You got a message for me? Well,

just let me have it and don't sing. I can't stand singing telegrams."

Alstein tried to wrest his hand free but he could not. The gun dropped dully to the wooden floor. The Oriental appeared from the far doorway in front of the .357 Magnum hole. Not a whisker on the long wispy beard was damaged.

Chiun moved quickly to Alstein and his hands darted around the bigger man's body like butterflies gone amok. He felt the metal spur taped to Alstein's stomach, but kept his hands moving for another moment before stepping back.

"Who sent you?" asked Remo, hopping down from the doorsill.

"Mr. Gordons."

"He's here on the island? Where is he?" asked Remo.

But Alstein's mouth gave forth no words. It opened and then filled with blood. The Master of Sinanju withdrew a long nail from the throat and like a spigot unplugged, Alstein's blood gushed forth from the puncture hole in his throat.

"What'd you do that for?" asked Remo. "What'd you do that for? He was going to tell us about Gordons."

"Hear ye, hear ye," wailed the Master of Sinanju. "Gordons, we do not wish your death. Sinanju yields. The world is big enough for both of us. Hail the House of Gordons."

"Now I know why you killed him," said Remo. "You don't want me to find Gordons."

Alstein writhed on the floor, his blood soaking his jacket, his arms flailing uselessly. Remo stepped away from the growing, seeping dark puddle.

"That's blood," said Remo. "You know how hard it

is to clean up blood? From dry wood, no less. You know how hard? Get him out of here."

But Chiun wailed again.

"No grief, no bill due do we hold against the glory of the House of Gordons. No wealth do we want. Sinanju yields."

"Shmuck," said Remo and with his good arm snared Alstein's belt and carried him at arm's length, so as not to get himself messed up, out to the porch where with one spinning heave he threw the body splashing into Magen's Bay.

"We got any Comet or Babbo or Fantastick in the house?" asked Remo. "Shmuck."

"Yield to Gordons. Peace we seek," said Chiun.

"Maybe some Lestoil?" said Remo.

In the Windward Hotel, the small television screen on a set without a case had transmitted Chiun's words of peace. The last picture it showed was of the sky. The fading morning stars seemed to be racing away, and then the picture shuddered, flashed an image of bubbles, and then only blackness and silence.

Jellicoe watched the set turn itself off. He shook his head and moaned. Sergeant Pitulski looked confused.

"I didn't see nothing. Just the door. The shot, the gook that should of gone down, and then the hand coming like it was suspended from up above, you know. You think they got some trick machinery in that house or something?"

"No," said Mr. Gordons. "Well, so much for metal. Now we try fire, Sergeant Pitulski."

"The Marines are ready to move out," said Pitulski.

"Stay more than an arm's length away," said Mr. Gordons. "If we go now, we may catch them in the house. Stay twenty-five yards away and hit the house

84

from there. I think I saw a clearing on the television transmission, so they won't have the advantage of places to hide to come up on you. This may be effective."

Driving to the house overlooking Magen's Bay, the three did not take the experimental roads Alstein had tried. They knew the best way, because they had watched him wander all night over the little TV set. As the now hot morning made breathing difficult in the car, Sergeant Pitulski wondered why Mr. Gordons wanted to accompany him.

"Because you drink. There is nothing more unreliable than a human being with alcohol in his bloodstream."

"I fight better drunk than sober," said Pitulski.

"A chemical illusion," said Mr. Gordons as he drove up winding Mafoli Avenue; down behind them they could see Charlotte Amalie at the foot of the rising hill, and the fine white cruise ships docked in the bay.

"May I ask why we want to kill those two?" said Jellicoe. "I mean if you want to tell us."

"I have no desire not to tell you. The one without the beard, which would indicate he was younger, has extraordinary strength. He damaged my left side. Now if he could do this, then either he or the bearded one, or both together, could destroy me. Correct?"

"Correct," said Jellicoe. "But the Oriental said he didn't want to. That was the one thing he made clear. That he didn't want to tangle with you."

" 'Tangle,' I take it, means battle," said Gordons. "That is one thing he said. Just because a person says something does not mean he will act upon it."

"But we had to go find them, didn't we?" asked Jellicoe.

"You are correct. That only indicates, however, that

they are not coming after me *now*," said Mr. Gordons.

"And from what I gathered, they don't want to come after you. At least not the old one who seems to get his way; he doesn't want to come after you at all, ever," said Jellicoe.

"Who gives a shit?" said Sergeant Pitulski.

"Will you shut up, you dummy?" said Jellicoe.

Mr. Gordons continued driving smoothly, apparently ignoring Pitulski.

"I too tend sixty-four percent positive, plus or minus eight percent, that the bearded one would avoid me. At least for now. And I too could avoid them."

"Then why are you, we, us, all of us trying to kill them?"

"Because it is optimum," said Mr. Gordons.

"I don't understand."

"If they are dead, my chances of survival improve. Therefore, I will kill them. In killing them, I will also become effective against anyone like them."

"All right, can I ask why? I mean, why do you want to become effective against them and people like them?"

"To maximize my survival."

"But there's got to be more of a reason. There's such a small chance you would ever meet people like them again. I mean, do you spend all your time just surviving?"

"Exactly," said Mr. Gordons.

"Doing nothing but surviving?"

"Surviving requires all my effort."

"How about love?" asked Jellicoe, desperately hoping to strike some emotion other than this computer-like insistence on only survival.

"Love has as many meanings as there are people,"

said Mr. Gordons. "It is not capable of programming," he added, and he turned up a narrow road that rose above Magen's Bay.

"There it is, Sergeant Pitulski," said Mr. Gordons as they stopped at a driveway which was cut into a clearing. In the center of the small clearing was a wooden house with a large hole in the front door where a doorknob might have been.

"Now this is how I want you to do it," said Mr. Gordons, as he strapped the flamethrower unit to Sergeant Pitulski's back and checked the nozzle end of the tube which fitted under his arm. "I don't want a direct spray that can be evaded. I want you to first set the far side of the house aflame, then move the flame around left in a circle that comes almost to your feet, and then keep going onward toward your right until the circle is closed. With the fire, you will make the flames fatter toward the house until we have a funeral fire."

Sergeant Pitulski said it wasn't the Marine way; Mr. Gordons said it was the way it would be done.

The first line of flame shot in an arch over the dry wooden house and the droplets caught and flared wherever they landed. In a surprisingly even circle, Sergeant Pitulski set the brush aflame and brought the circle to a close, but, as he did so, he lost the exact sighting of the house in the rising flame. He stepped back to higher ground and haphazardly filled in the center of the circle, but such was the dryness of the brush and wood of the house that the whole area went roaring up under the infusion of liquid flame. Sergeant Pitulski backed away from the roaring heat.

"Well, that's it," said Jellicoe, watching from the front seat as Mr. Gordons got back into the car.

"Invalid," said Mr. Gordons and started the car with a roar and spun it around and down the road. As Jellicoe looked back, he saw two figures, one in a barely smoking kimono and the other with what appeared to be a bandaged arm, flip Sergeant Pitulski into his own pyre. The fatty body made nary a pop on its way to crispness.

Mr. Gordons's driving amazed Jellicoe. He took corners at just the maximum possible speed, and soon he was on the open highway, but looking behind, Jellicoe could see that the young man with the damaged shoulder was not only keeping up with them, but was gaining on them, driving at a speed so incredible that he seemed to churn above the concrete road itself.

"On with your water gear, On with it. It's in the back seat," said Mr. Gordons. "It's your one chance for survival. Quickly." Jellicoe struggled with the suit as they speeded along the bumpy mountain road, but gave up and settled for the tanks and the mask and fins. Into the small gate at Magen's Bay Beach, Mr. Gordons spun the car, skidding to avoid a large beach house. There were shrieks from bathers. To avoid a tree, Mr. Gordons ran over a little toddler. Down the beach, he braked the car to a skidding, sandy stop.

"Out. The water is your only chance. Quickly, into it."

With his flippers on, Jellicoe could only penguin walk toward the water, but once in it, his flippers began to work, and he got his rubber mouthpiece set in his teeth and turned on the tank and blessedly moved along the sandy bottom.

Magen's Bay was not deep near the shore so Jellicoe swam directly out to sea. He was at home here in these clear waters, at home because what he feared was on land. And he thought that perhaps when man first left the sea, crawled up in that primitive state onto land, he had done so to escape what might be in the sea.

At forty feet deep, his back flipper caught in something and he turned to dislodge it. When he did, he saw the young man with the injured shoulder. His face was very calm.

In the water, Jellicoe worked on one chance, holding the man down without air. Surprisingly, the man did not resist. Jellicoe put his arms around the neck and the man was motionless, this man whose only name Jellicoe knew was Remo.

Jellicoe saw no bubbles and the man did not resist. So Jellicoe held for ten minutes, then released, and rose toward the glittering surface, having earned, he thought, his hundred thousand dollars.

But he stopped short of the light above him. Something was tugging at his flippers. It was Remo. And he tugged downward and when his face was level with Jellicoe's face mask, he smiled and removed the mouthpiece connected to the air from the tanks behind the diver. And as water flooded Jellicoe's lungs, he had a strange thought: he had never had a chance to get rid of the metal spur. And then there was something even more strange. Under water, he thought he heard this Remo say something, something that sounded like:

"That's the biz, sweetheart."

On a cliff over Magen's Bay, Mr. Gordons had stopped to watch the combat beneath clear water.

"That makes negative for water as well as fire as well as metal," he said softly to himself. "If only I were more creative. This new program I acquired at O'Hare Airport, it can be improved. But how?"

He heard something move in the brush fifty yards away and although he could not see it, he could track its direction. It moved faster than men could run and when it emerged from the bushes it stopped. In robes singed dark at the edges was the Oriental.

"Mr. Gordons, why do you persist?" asked Chiun. "What endeavors do we, my son and I, endanger of yours? Tell us so we may avoid them."

"Your existence is what endangers me."

"How? We seek not to assault you."

"So you say."

"So I show. I keep my distance. Without your lackeys near you, I still keep my distance."

"Would you move against me? Attack," said Mr. Gordons.

"No," said the Master of Sinanju. "You attack me, if you dare."

"I have already. With those lackeys."

"Attack me with your person," defied Chiun.

"Are you a person?" asked Mr. Gordons.

"Yes. The most skilled of persons," said Chiun.

"I wondered. I wondered how you knew that he who attacks with himself first, gives away his patterns of attack and becomes the more vulnerable," said Mr. Gordons.

"The question is how do you know, white man," said Chiun.

"It is my nature. By nature, I react."

"The gun and the fire were not reactions," said Chiun.

"A bit of my new creativity," said Mr. Gordons. "It is something I need more of."

"Thank you," said the Master of Sinanju and

disappeared back into the thick growth covering the hill rising above Magen's Bay. Neither he nor Remo would have to wait for a later generation of the Masters of Sinanju. Mr. Gordons had given himself away.

CHAPTER SIX

"We attack," said Chiun, and Remo shrugged in confusion for he saw no enemy, as he had seen no enemy when they had left St. Thomas and Chiun had said "We attack," as he had seen no enemy in the NASA Space Center in Houston when Chiun had said "We attack," as he had seen no enemy when the office of public relations at NASA had said:

"The research on the creativity component has pretty well been given up because of cutbacks in the program. It's now non-operative."

"Aha," Chiun had said.

"Does that mean it's closed down?" Remo asked.

"Pretty much," said the public relations man.

"We understood you the first time," Chiun said.

"Horsefeathers," said Remo. According to a brochure on unmanned space flight that they got from the public relations man, the component they sought had been developed in Cheyenne, Wyoming, and by the time their plane had landed, both Remo and Chiun were exhausted from the pressures of flight upon systems more finely tuned and more sensitive than the average person's.

The Wilkins Laboratory, as it was called, was a three-story building, rising from a flat grassy plain, as though someone had stuck an isolated box on a bare floor. It was dusk when Remo and Chiun arrived: all three floors of the laboratory were lit.

"Doesn't look like there's been any cutback here," said Remo.

"We attack," said Chiun.

"What the hell do we attack? First you want to run, then after Mr. Gordons comes after us, you want to attack and I don't see what we're attacking."

"His weakness. He gave us his weakness."

"I already saw his weakness. He moves funny. If I hadn't thought that was him in the water in Magen's Bay, I could have gotten him back in St. Thomas. He decoyed me."

"Wrong," said Chiun. "He bracketed us. To find out what is, he found out what wasn't. Neither metal, nor fire, nor water worked against us. He found this out without risk to himself. But in his arrogance, he told us that he would not leave us alone, so we must attack."

"But you said a future generation, and only when they knew Mr. Gordons's flaws."

"We are that generation. He told me on the cliffs. He lacks creativity. Now this is a place that designs machines for creativity. Mr. Gordons knew about it. That is why he wanted that thingamajig you gave him at the airport in that dirty city. Now we are here. And we attack. You will, of course, take care of the details."

"Well, how are we going to get an attack out of creativity?"

"I do not know machines," said Chiun. "I am not Japanese or white. That's your job. All whites know machines."

"All Orientals don't know Sinanju; why should all whites know machines? I don't know anything about machines."

"Then ask someone. You will learn it quickly."

"I can maybe change a sparkplug, Little Father."

"See. I told you. You know machines. All whites know machines. You fixed the machine with the offensive drama."

"That was just threading a movie projector reel."

"And it will be just figuring out an attack that uses a machines that makes creativity."

"These are space-age computers, Chiun. Not movie projectors."

"We attack," said Chiun, advancing on the building.

"How do we know we'll ever see Gordons again?" asked Remo.

"Aha," said Chiun, clutching a lump of lead that he wore on a thong around his neck. "We know. Inside here is the secret," but he would say no more because while he knew Remo would be good with machines, because all whites were, he was still afraid that Remo might somehow find a way to break the metal spur by which Gordons could track them down. Chiun would keep it wrapped in lead until it was time to call Gordons to join them.

When they reached the front door of the laboratory, a woman's voice, husky with too many cigarettes and dry martinis, asked, "Who's there?" Remo looked for the woman but did not see her.

"I said who's there?" The voice did not sound as if it came over a speaker but when the voice repeated the question, Chiun spotted the source. It was a speak-

94

er, apparently of incredible fidelity, without the ring or vibration of normal speakers.

"The Master of Sinanju and pupil," said Chiun.

"Put your hands on the door."

Chiun placed his long-nailed hands flat on the metal door. Remo followed, keeping alert to any possible attack from behind.

"All right, you perspire. You can come in."

The door slid to the right, revealing a lighted passageway. As they entered, Remo and Chiun cursorily checked above and alongside the door. No one.

The passageway smelled strangely like a bar.

The door closed behind them.

"All right. Talk. Who sent you?"

"We're here about a creativity program," said Remo.

"I thought so, you bastards. The rat doesn't dare come here himself. How much did he offer to pay you? I'll top it."

"In gold?" asked Chiun.

"Cash," said the voice.

"If it were gold, the House of Sinanju is at this moment seeking employ."

"Sinanju? That's a town in Korea, right. Just a second. Hold on. Okay, Sinanju, North Korea, House of. A secretive society of assassins, known for exceptional ruthlessness and willingness to hire itself out to any buyer. Said to be the sun source of the martial arts, but little is known of its existence. Nothing is known of its ways or even if it is not just some ancient tale used by the dynasties of China to frighten people into submission. You don't look that frightening, fella."

"I am not. I am but a vessel of humility come to your great house, oh, beautiful maiden of the machines," said Chiun, who whispered to Remo, "She probably has no gold. Do not take paper money."

95

"I heard that. Come on in. You look okay."

A door slid open in the apparently seamless wall to their right. Sitting at a little cocktail table with shelves of liquor behind her was a blonde with a body that could make a priest burn his collar. Her breasts protruded in mammoth declaration of milk potential, reaching out to the limits of a stretching white smock. Her waist nosedived in and roared out at the hips again. A short light blue skirt revealed smooth white thighs.

When Remo finally noticed her eyes, he saw they were blue. And bloodshot.

"What can I offer you to drink?" she said. "Sit down."

"Ah, sweet delicate flower," said Chiun. "What soaring heights your presence imparts to our humble hearts."

"Glad to meet you," said Remo.

"You're lying through your teeth," she said, pointing a martini glass at Remo. "You can't bullshit me. You like my boobs or my brains." Then she pointed to Chiun. "You, on the other hand, are on the level. You're real. Tell your phony friend not to lay it on."

"He is but ignorant of true sensitivity. True graciousness of which you are the embodiment, fair lady."

"All right. But make sure he keeps his hands to himself," she said. "What'll you have to drink? Hey, Mr. Seagrams. Make it snappy with the booze."

From behind the bar, a liquor cart rolled out, with glasses tinkling as it went.

"Just water, thank you," said Chiun.

"Same for me," said Remo.

"Where'd you meet this wet blanket?" the woman asked Chiun.

"I have my difficulties with him, as you see."

96

"Difficulties. I can tell you about difficulties."

Metal trays on metal arms moved and shuffled bottles and glasses and ice. To make the water, one tray melted ice cubes.

"These machines are driving me to the brink of schizophrenia," she said. "You program them and program them and then they misfunction. If I programmed Mr. Seagrams once to offer drinks whenever someone enters, I programmed him a hundred times. You give a drink or an explanation why you can't. I don't know why it should be so difficult."

"I know your problems," said Chiun, nodding to Remo. "But I thought machines never forget."

"Well, it's not really the machines. It's that the programming has to be incredibly subtle. I'm Vanessa Carlton, Dr. Carlton. Maybe you've heard of me."

"Ah, the famous Dr. Carlton," said Chiun.

Remo looked up at the ceiling and sighed. Chiun not only hadn't heard of Dr. Carlton, he still hadn't heard of Newton, Edison, and Einstein.

"Unmanned space flight. We do the computer components here which are the brains of it. A little freshening on the martini, Mr. Seagrams," she said, and the cart sent out a shiny arm that brought the martini glass to a large bottle of gin, filled it with two clear shots and then added a small spray of vermouth.

"You want something to eat?"

"Some brown rice would be nice," said Chiun.

"Hey. Johnny Walker. Some brown rice. A hundred grams. And don't let it stick this time. Where was I?"

"You being the brains of the unmanned space program," said Remo.

"An unmanned space program is nothing without its compost," said Chiun.

"Computer components. You're right. Well, if
97

NASA were running Columbus's expedition, they would have withheld the rudder to save costs. I mean it. They don't spring for spit. Hey, this martini is good. You're getting better looking. What's your name?"

"Remo. I look good when people are sober, too."

"I'm not drunk, shithead," said Dr. Carlton and took a good long swallow on her martini.

"Where was I?"

"Columbus being denied a rudder," said Remo. A door on the far side of the room opened and a small tray on wheels came rolling to the little table. On top were two steaming bowls. The tray served them onto the desk with the same metallic arm.

"Dammit," shrieked Dr. Carlton. "You burned the rice." She kicked the cart across the room. "Dammit. Now you know why I drink. These machines."

"Rudders," said Remo.

"Right. Well, that's taken care of, anyway," said Dr. Carlton, unbuttoning one button on the top of her blouse and airing a glorious crevice. "But do you know what they did? You know what they do all the time? First they give me a ton of money. They tell me to make this and buy that and try this. Do you know that I've got a rocket ready to launch, built right into the ground here at these labs? My own rocket. Right here. They insisted on it. So they give you all this money and you get staff and materials and you get started, and then they tell you no more money, and you've got to fire your staff, and the materials you bought gather dust on the shelves. Ah, piss on them."

"Of course," said Chiun, and Remo knew he was acting because he abhorred Western profanity, especially in women.

"What we have come about," Chiun said, "is a

98

creativity. How does one make creativity out of a machine?"

"Aha," said Dr. Carlton. "Come with me. You want to know about creativity, well, I'll show you. It has to do with survival," and she grabbed Remo's arm on her way to her feet and held on as she led them into a room the size of a stadium. Rising to the arched beamed ceiling were frontplates of machines, dials so high Remo looked for elevators for people to get up to read them. Three stories high and Remo assumed that was only the control panel.

"That, my friends, is Mr. Daniels. I have christened him Mr. Jack Daniels. You couldn't send him into space, could you?"

She led them into the room. A man stood to the left, his back to them, looking up at the machine.

Quietly, Dr. Carlton walked up behind him, then gave a tremendous uppercut swing of her right toe. It caught the man in the buttocks and propelled him across the room where he flopped, thwack, head first against the floor.

"Stay out of the way, Mr. Smirnoff," Dr. Carlton yelled. The figure of the man did not move, but lay awkwardly awry on the hard stone floor. "Hahaha-hahahaha." Dr. Carlton's laugh echoed through the high-domed room like the shrieks of a malevolent bird. She turned and saw Remo and Chiun staring at her in silence.

"Hey," she said quickly, "don't take it so hard. That's not a person. It's a dummy. Mr. Smirnoff. We use it for measurements in the lab here. Somebody must have left it out in the middle of the floor. Now where were we? Oh, yes, creativity."

Dr. Carlton walked closer to the control panels, Chiun and Remo on her heels. "Jack Daniels here is a computer. Do you know what a synapse is?"

Remo looked blank. Chiun said, "Not nearly as much as you do, gracious and brilliant doctor." He whispered behind his hand to Remo, "A synapse is when they tell you what happened in yesterday's story. But let her tell us. It will make her feel smart."

"A synapse," said Dr. Carlton, "is a junction of two brain cells. The human brain has more than two billion of them. Out of all those junctions comes what we know as intelligence. Mr. Jack Daniels is the closest we've got to it. He's got two billion synapses, too. If it weren't for transistors and miniaturization, to have that many he'd have to be as big as Central Park. Thanks to transistors, I've been able to shrink him down to a little less than the size of a city block."

"Let her babble," Chiun whispered. "A synapse is a retelling, but shorter, of a story."

"That's a synopsis, Chiun, not a synapse," said Remo.

"You whites all stick together," Chiun muttered.

Vanessa Carlton was looking up at the control panel. Remo saw that her nostrils were pinched, her lips set in a thin straight line, her bosom rising and falling like boiling pudding.

"Look at it," she said. "A city-block-sized cretin. An imbecile."

"Send it back to the manufacturer," said Remo.

"I *am* the manufacturer," she said. "I've put into this goddam thing everything I know."

"Maybe you don't know enough," said Remo.

"No, Browneyes. I know plenty. A grade-A, certifiable, Mensa-type, high-level genius."

"If she is so smart, surely she would know what a synapse is," whispered Chiun.

Vanessa Carlton did not hear him. She went on,

100

talking more to the computer than to either man. "You know what a genius is? A genius knows when something is impossible. My greatest act of creative genius is to know that it's impossible to create creativity."

"Come again?" said Remo.

"That's something else," she said. "Not again but just once. I'd love to. But get sex off your mind. God, why are you men always interested in nothing but sex. Jugs. Butts. That's all you ever think about. I'm trying to talk sense to you and all you can think of is female orgasm."

"Do not worry yourself with him," said Chiun. "He is untrained and couthless."

Vanessa Carlton nodded in agreement. "Anyway," she said, "I've given up. I've programmed my machines for everything. For speech. For movement. For strength. For adaptability. For analysis. For survival. I've gone further than anyone else ever has gone. But I just can't build creativity into them."

"So what?" asked Remo.

She shook her head at what she regarded as rampant stupidity. "You must be good in the sack, Browneyes, 'cause you ain't too shiny any other way."

"Call me Remo," said Remo.

"Fine. And you can call me Dr. Carlton. If we could have designed creativity into a spaceship computer, three unmanned probes that we lost would still be working. A computer, you see, works fine when everything is predictable."

"Weather changes. Malfunctions. Meteor showers, all those things that knock out spaceships. They don't seem very predictable," said Remo.

"But they are. Variables are the most predictable things of all. You just program in different possi-

101

bilities and teach the computer what to do in response to them. But what you can't do is teach a machine to respond to something unique, something that wasn't programmed in. Or to do anything unique, for that matter. You can't find a computer that's going to paint a Gioconda smile on the Mona Lisa."

In Remo's ear, Chiun whispered, "That is a picture of a fat Italian woman with a silly smirk."

"Thanks, Chiun," said Remo.

"You've seen computers play chess," the woman said. "You can program them with a million different games played by a thousand different masters. And the first time they run up against a player who makes a move that's got brilliance in it, a move that's not in their program, they start to babble like idiots. They not only can't create, they can't function in the face of creativity. What a drag."

They were interrupted by the cart called Mr. Seagrams rolling in silently and taking Dr. Carlton's martini glass from her hand. It mixed a fresh martini and extended it to her. She took it wordlessly and the cart went into reverse and rolled back toward the door. Dr. Carlton took a vicious sip.

"What a drag," she repeated. "My contribution to scientific history is going to be to say that there's a limit to man's creativity. He cannot create its duplicate. An interesting paradox, don't you think? Man is so unlimited that he meets his limit when he tries to duplicate himself. The Carlton Paradox."

"What is she talking about?" asked Remo.

"Quiet," hissed Chiun. "She is teaching us how to combat Mr. Gordons."

"Well, if you can't create creativity, what was this creativity program you put together for NASA a little while ago?" asked Remo.

102

"It was the best I could do," she said. "A five-year-old's creativity. It's kind of creativity at random. A five-year-old can't focus. Neither could my creativity program. You couldn't put it to use to solve any specific problem because you never knew when it was going to be creative."

"Then why'd the government take it?" asked Remo.

"Why not? They might get lucky. Suppose it decided to get creative at just the right time, at just the moment some unforeseen problem arises on a mission? Whammo, it could save a flight. It couldn't hurt and it might help."

"And that's the program they gave Mr. Gordons," Remo said.

The martini glass dropped from Vanessa Carlton's hand and shattered on the stone floor, splashing the liquor upon her mini-skirted legs, but she was oblivious to it.

"What did you say?" She stared hard at Remo.

"That was the program Mr. Gordons got his hands on," said Remo.

"No," she said in disbelief. "No. They weren't stupid enough to . . ."

"Sure were," said Remo cheerily.

"Do they know what they've done? Do they have any idea?"

"No," said Remo. "Neither do we. That's why we're here. To talk to you about Mr. Gordons. Just who is he anyway?"

"Mr. Gordons is the most dangerous . . . man in the world."

"He used to work here?" Remo asked.

"You might say that. And if they give him creativity, even a little of it, he could run amok. Creativity

103

might just tell him to kill everybody because everybody's a threat to him."

"And then what?"

"And then a lot of people will die. Who are you anyway? You're not from NASA, are you?"

"Let me handle this, Remo," said Chiun. He turned to Dr. Carlton. "No, dear lady, we are just two humble people attracted by your brilliance and who have come to learn at your feet."

"You know, old fella, I don't think I trust you anymore."

Chiun nodded. "It is best to be cautious. I myself never trust anyone under seventy. But you can trust us."

"Not until you tell me who you are," said Dr. Carlton.

Remo interrupted Chiun. "We're from the government. We've got to track down Gordons and put him out of commission before he floods the country with counterfeits. Now we need your help." He stopped. Dr. Carlton was laughing.

"What's so funny?" Remo asked.

"You can't put Mr. Gordons out of commission," she said.

"Maybe," said Remo. "But for openers, you might just tell us where his printing plant is. If I can get to that . . ." Again he stopped. Dr. Carlton was laughing uproariously, her eyes filled with tears. Remo tried again to talk, but could barely hear himself over her high-pitched gales of laughter.

"Dammit, this is serious," he tried to say. He looked at Chiun. Chiun said, "We will learn nothing more here today. What can we learn from a woman who doesn't even know what a synapse is?" He looked hurt.

They walked toward the door, retreating from the peals of laughter that reverberated in the room as Dr. Carlton went from hilarity to hysteria. Silently, they trudged down the hallway toward the metal front door. As they reached the sliding panel, Remo said, "Dammit, Chiun, I'm not taking this."

"What are you going to do?"

"Attack," Remo said. "Attack. Wait outside for me."

Chiun shrugged and went out through the automatic door. Remo was alone in the corridor. He walked noiselessly back toward the main computer room.

The door to the room was still open, but there was no more laughter from within. Inside, instead, Remo heard the drone of voices. The female voice was Vanessa Carlton's.

". . . you must change all the lock combinations and install additional electronic detectors. Do you understand?"

The male voice that answered was dull and thin sounding. "I understand. Anything you wish, Doctor."

"Then do it."

At that moment, Remo entered the room.

Standing before the control panel where he had left her was Dr. Carlton. But in front of her stood a man. He wore a gray business suit. Remo looked to the left. The dummy that she had kicked to the floor was gone. It too had worn a gray suit. Both Dr. Carlton and the man turned as Remo entered the room, the man's eyes following Dr. Carlton's startled gaze. Jerkily, it took a step forward toward Remo. Its eyes were clear, but seemed unfocussed, yet locked on Remo with a look he would have sworn was hate had it been seen anywhere but on that expressionless face.

105

"No, Mr. Smirnoff," said Vanessa Carlton. "Do what I said about the locks."

The man stopped his advance toward Remo. His metallic voice answered again. "As you wish, Doctor."

Remo watched as the creature moved toward him, walking deliberately like a man recovering from a paralyzing stroke who has found that his body no longer does the simple basic things naturally, and each act is the direct result of will. Remo stepped aside, watching Mr. Smirnoff's hands waiting for a move against him, and then realizing he was a fool: would robots tip their moves with their hands? But Mr. Smirnoff slid past him silently, without a glance, and went through the door.

After he had left, Dr. Carlton spoke. "So what now, Browneyes?"

"You can start anywhere."

"Where's your friend?"

"Waiting outside."

"How much do you know about Mr. Gordons?" she asked.

"I know one thing now."

"Which is?"

"He's not human," Remo said.

Vanessa Carlton nodded. "No, he's not. But you'll probably wish he were."

"You in the business of making robots?" Remo said.

"No. Spaceship components." Vanessa Carlton put down her new martini glass, and, stepping lightly over the glass chips from her dropped last drink, went to the computer console. From a small cabinet in the front of the computer, she took out a handful of electrical leads. Carefully, she began to separate the tangled wires as she talked.

"It was just more efficient to make them in humanoid

106

shape," she said. "It allowed them to understand better what will face a crewmember on a later manned mission. What is a problem for a six-foot astronaut might not be a problem for a foot-square metal box. So I used the humanoid shape."

"Why didn't you use it on your rolling bartender there, Mr. Seagrams?"

"He was just an early experiment in getting computers to respond to voice signals." She began to lay the electrical leads out, as she separated each one from the cluster, onto the long table in front of the computer panel. "I worked out that problem. Not only could they hear and understand but I made it possible for them to talk. I programmed them for increasingly more difficult tasks. But . . ." She shook her head sadly. "No creativity. Let's face it, Browneyes, machines don't mean a thing if they ain't got that swing. Mr. Gordons was the closest I've come."

Remo perched on the edge of a chair, watching Dr. Carlton, follow her bouncing breasts around the table, stretching wires out to their full length.

"What's the difference between Gordons, say, and Mr. Smirnoff there?"

"Night and day," the blonde said. "Mr. Smirnoff is programmed to obey and to do whatever pleases me. He's just a dedicated mechanical butler. But Mr. Gordons, now he's different."

"How?"

"He's an assimilator and fabricator. It was a major breakthrough. Mr. Gordons is the entire American military-industrial complex gathered up in one. He can take anything and make anything out of it. Put a chair in front of him and he can make paper out of it or an exact replica of the tree it came from. Given raw materials, he can duplicate anything. If you must know,

107

that man-like look of his, he created it all himself out of plastics and metals."

She had all the leads separated now and she raised herself up on the conference table, sitting on its edge. She took one of the electrical leads and began to fasten it with tape to her left temple.

"So what makes him different?" asked Remo. "So he's a strong robot that looks like a man. Why's he coming after us?"

Dr. Carlton shook her head with the dismay of the specialist trying to explain the complicated to the layman. "It's his program," she said. "Look. Here is how it went. The government wanted a creativity program. I couldn't give them one. It looked like the government was going to close down our lab. I needed to come up with something. I came up with survival."

"Survival," said Remo.

"Right. Mr. Gordons is programmed for survival. Nothing else matters to him except how to survive." Left electrode in place, she began to tape another electrode to her right temple. "Somehow, he must have gotten the idea that you and your friend threaten his chances for survival. I guess he decided he must get rid of you to survive. Remember, that's all he knows."

"What did the government say about it?"

"Well, that was my thought," said Dr. Carlton. "If I couldn't design creative intelligence, I might be able to get practically the same result if I could program a robot to survive. That was why they wanted creative intelligence anyway: to help a spaceship survive. I thought a survival mechanism might work just as well as a creatively intelligent one."

"So?"

108

"So," she said bitterly, "I couldn't convince the government. They didn't want anything to do with it. They gave me three months to come up with creativity."

The two head electrodes were in place and Dr. Carlton now began attaching a third to her left wrist.

"So I came back here and told the staff we were in trouble. That it looked like the lab wouldn't survive. Mr. Gordons heard me. That night, he devised a human form for himself and ran out. I haven't seen him since."

"Well, didn't you tell anybody? Give them a warning?"

"Warn them about what? Remember, when Mr. Gordons was here, he was just a machine. He looked kind of like a butter churn atop a hospital cart. He took human form as a survival mechanism when he was leaving. He assimilated plastic and metal and redesigned himself. But I've never seen him. I don't know what he looks like. That's why I have such security here. I've been afraid he'll come back, if he decides there's something here that he needs, and I for one wouldn't want to try to stop him."

She had finished strapping the electrodes on both wrists and now beckoned Remo to her with a finger.

"Come here, Browneyes."

Remo walked to where Vanessa Carlton sat on the edge of the table. She put her arms around his chest. "For all I know, you might be Mr. Gordons. That's why I'm going to have to test you."

She stretched up, placed her lips on his, kissed hard, and then fell backward onto the table, pulling Remo down with her.

"I don't know what it is about you," she said. "It's sure not your brain, but something turns me on. Make love to me." Her wired wrists pulled open the front buttons of her blouse, then slid her skirt up the few inches necessary for it to clear her hips.

"I turn most women on. But you got enough wires on you to turn yourself on and off like a lamp."

"That's your civilian review board. For when you fail like every other man. Get on with it."

Remo reached a hand between them, began working it gently, and then jumped from the table when a voice boomed: "A little to the left." The booming sound reverberated throughout the room. Remo looked around. The room was empty.

"What the hell was that?"

"Our computer, Mr. Daniels. He's going to keep you posted on how you're doing."

"Oh, crap," said Remo.

"Get back up here," said Dr. Carlton.

"Your soft compliant ways are really the way to a man's heart," Remo said.

"Do your duty. Who do you work for anyway?"

"The government. The Secret Service," Remo lied. "We're after Gordons's counterfeiting operation."

This time he put his right hand between them again but he would not be dictated to by a computer so he moved his hand not left, but even farther to the right.

The computer did not complain this time. Instead it seemed to hum plaintively.

"To the left, huh?" Remo mumbled under his breath. "We'll see."

He moved his hand even farther right. The computer's humming became a moan. Remo brought his left hand up around under Vanessa Carlton's satiny flanks. The moaning increased. The computer's muffled roar said, "Oh, yes. Oh, yes."

110

Remo joined with Dr. Carlton on the table. Roaring over all came the computer's metallic voice saying, "That's wonderful. That's wonderful. Magic. Magic."

Remo was uncomfortable. It was like performing in front of witnesses. And the fact that Mr. Daniels, the computer, had a baritone voice didn't help either. Annoyed, Remo set to work.

"Magic, magic, magic, magic," said the computer. Its voice began to change. From baritone to tenor.

"Magic, magic, magic, magic." From tenor to soprano, then going faster and faster. "Magic, magic, magic, magic." So fast some syllables became indistinct.

The word "magic" was repeated over and over again and then the machine began to babble. "Ma-mama-ma-gic-gic-gic-gic. Gic-ma. Gic-ma. Magic-ma Gic-ma-gic." Then it giggled, a high squeaky castrati giggle that grew longer and higher and more shrill and changed into a wail.

"Oh, balls," said Remo and yanked the tape electrodes from Vanessa Carlton's temples. The computer stopped in mid-shriek, replaced by Vanessa Carlton's very authentic soprano moan and babble.

"Magic-ma, Gic-magic . . . giggle, giggle . . . gic-magic-ma."

And then he felt her spasm and moan and he felt like smacking her around and her smartass computer, too. He raised himself and backed away from her, and she said, "Oh, Remo. Such pleasure. It's never been like that. Oh, wow. That might replace alcohol, if you're not careful. Such pleasure."

Remo turned to begin straightening his clothes and looked up to find Mr. Smirnoff standing silently inside the door, his robot's eyes fixed on Dr. Carlton who lay, well-pleasured on the table, babbling: "Wonderful, I'm so happy, wonderful, magic, happy, pleasure."

Clothes straightened, Remo turned back to her. "All right, now where does Mr. Gordons keep his counterfeiting equipment?"

The question started her laughing. "I don't know anything about counterfeiting," she said. Her laugh did not sound authentic. Remo chose not to press the subject any further. For now.

"Any tips? How do I get him?"

"Remember. He can't create any better than a five-year-old. Flashy but inconsistent." She sat up and began smoothing her clothes. "That's his weakness. He would've been easy for you if those idiots in Washington hadn't given him the creativity program."

Remo nodded and turned to leave. Vanessa called him back. "Remo?"

He turned.

"What does he look like anyway?"

"Mr. Gordons?"

She nodded."

Remo described Mr. Gordons. His height, over six feet, sandy blondish hair, thin lips, the blue eyes. Halfway through, she began to laugh.

"I had wondered where he got his model."

"And?"

"He got it from a picture on my desk. Mr. Gordons copied my father's looks."

CHAPTER SEVEN

"I don't like this," said Remo, looking out the window of the 747 racing eastward toward New York.

"What is this thing you do not like?" asked Chiun, sitting peacefully in an aisle seat, his hands holding onto the leaden lump strung around his neck. "Keep an eye on that wing," he added quickly.

"Smith calling us back east. It must be important."

"Why? Because Emperor Smith calls? What does that mean? It might just be that he has gone mad again. He has taken leave of his senses before, if you remember. When he was in the place called Cincinnati and you were trying to find him in the place called Pittsburgh?"

"All right, all right, all right," said Remo. "Let's just drop it. I'm glad anyway that you've agreed to go back to work for him."

"Was there ever any doubt? You and I must attack. He will pay us to attack. We should not take his gold? We would be as mad as he probably is, just as he was when he was in the place called Cincinnati and you were trying to . . ."

Remo tuned Chiun out and stared out the window again.

When they met Smith, several hours later, he had not gone mad. He awaited them in a basement vault beneath New York's largest bank building. His face was drawn and pinched, more lemony than usual.

"What's up, Smitty, that's so important?" asked Remo breezily.

"Have you gotten any lead on where Mr. Gordons is printing the money?"

Remo shook his head.

"Then we're in serious trouble."

"When aren't we? Do you know that every time I've seen you in ten years, we've been in trouble? The sky is always falling. And this is the worst one of all, of course. The almighty dollar is in danger."

It was Smith's turn to shake his head. "Not the dollar," he said. "You."

"See," said Chiun to Remo. "It is not so important after all. It is just you."

That, however, Remo decided, made it very important. "What about me?" he said.

Smith handed forward a yellow slip of paper. "This came," he said.

Remo took the paper. Before reading what was on it, he handled the small sheet between his fingertips. It was exceptionally thin, thinner than onionskin, but stiff and strong, crisper than bond. He had never felt paper quite like it.

He looked down at it and read the printed note:

TO THOSE AMONG WHOM THERE MAY BE CONCERN:
Hello is all right. Please be advised that unless the head of one high probability Remo is delivered

114

to me that a billion dollars in money will be disbursed and dispersed—it is interesting how two similar words have totally different meanings but in this case both are correctly used, a fact of which I am proud—on an American city without warning. This is a serious promise. I'd offer you a drink but it is impossible through the mail. With best wishes, I am, sincerely, Mr. Gordons.

The note appeared to be typewritten but instead of the right edges of all the lines being uneven, as they would have if they been typed normally, the right margin was straight as if the note had been set in type on a linotype machine. Remo turned the paper over and felt the raised dots where the typed periods had pressed through the paper.

"What do you think?" Smith asked.

"Pretty smooth typing job," Remo said. "The right margin is perfectly even. Look at this, Chiun. A perfectly even margin. But it was done by a typewriter. I never saw a typewriter that could justify lines like that."

"Remo, will you stop it?" said Smith heatedly. "We're not here to talk about Mr. Gordons's typing."

"You're jealous. I bet you can't type a margin like that, and Mr. Gordons can. Come to think of it, you should be able to, 'cause you're both the same. Robots."

Smith's eyes rose in surprise. "Robots?"

"Right. Robots. No flesh and blood. He's just farther advanced than you 'cause he can type good. All you can do is play with your computers. Where did you go wrong, Smitty?"

"Chiun," said Smith. "Is this correct? Is Mr. Gordons a robot?"

"Yes," said Chiun. "We knew it all the time."

"*We* knew it? How did *we* know it?" demanded Remo.

"I am corrected," said Chiun. "*We* didn't know it. I knew it."

"Tell him how," said Remo. "Tell him how you knew. Tell him how I found out for you."

"Remo confirmed, but I knew. When a man does not walk like a man or talk like a man or act like a man, it is time to think he is perhaps not a man."

Remo saw Smith looking at him for added explanation. He shrugged. "I don't know. Some diddle-daddle stuff with Dr. Vanessa Carlton. She makes computer things for rockets. Mr. Gordons was some kind of survival computer. When it heard her say that the lab was going to be shut down because of no more government money, it dolled itself up like a man and ran away. 'Cause that's all it knows how to do, survive. And then of course the stupid government changed its mind and renewed the money for the lab anyway."

"The government never did change its mind," Smith said. "It stopped funding Dr. Carlton two months ago."

"Oh, who cares?" Remo said. "Anyway, that robot's running around loose now wondering what it has to do to survive. It thinks it's got it tough; it should try being a housewife with these prices."

"Technically, I guess, he is an android," Smith said.

"No. He's a robot," said Remo.

"A robot is a recognizable machine. An android is humanoid, that is, a robot that looks and acts human."

"All right, have it your own way. An android. Does that solve your problem?"

"The problem is still you. No one except me of course knows exactly who you are and what you do.

116

But some of the people at Treasury who have met you think we should give Mr. Gordons what he wants. That opinion might carry some weight with the President."

"Forsythe, right?" said Remo. Smith nodded.

Chiun played with the three-way switch on a lamp, changing it from dim to bright to brightest to off, dim to bright to brightest to off, rhythmically plunging the room into darkness.

"Suppose the President says do it?" asked Remo.

Smith shrugged. Chiun broke the small switch off the lamp.

"Where's my head supposed to be delivered?" Remo asked.

"It's supposed to be left in a litter basket at the Eastern Airlines desk at Dulles Airport, any night after 3 A.M. Gordons called Forsythe with the message. If you could only find the printing operation."

Chiun rose with the light switch in his hand. "Remo, let us leave Emperor Smith to his thoughts now." He put a hand on Remo's elbow and guided him from the room. "Do not talk anymore to him," Chiun warned. "He is crazy again."

CHAPTER EIGHT

Chiun insisted that he must see Forsythe immediately. Remo said that he did not care if he never saw Forsythe again. Chiun said that this showed only that Remo was stupid and knew nothing about nothing, but what could one expect of a white who was just like all other whites, even to his pasty complexion and stupid big feet and hands and thick wrists and no brains.

"The inferior always act alike. They think it will give them strength. But many fools, even together, are still fools."

"Enough, already," said Remo. He would talk no more and he sulked when they got into the taxicab, vowing not to tell Chiun where Forsythe's office was.

Chiun told the cabdriver, "Take us to Mr. Forsythe's office."

"Wha?" said the driver.

"Mr. Forsythe's office. He is a very important man. You must know him." He leaned forward and whispered confidentially, "He is white like you."

"Buddy, I don't know no Forsythe."

"I will describe him for you. He is ugly and stupid. A typical specimen."

The driver looked to Remo for help. Remo said nothing. Chiun said, "What is the ugliest building in this ugly city?"

"That's easy. They got this building for the Treasury that looks like a tomb."

"Take us there," said Chiun, sitting back comfortably on the seat. To Remo he said, "Where else would Forsythe be?"

The Treasury Building looked like a tomb because it was designed after a tomb—the tomb of Mausolus who had given his name through the ages to the type of building known as a mausoleum.

Chiun waited while Remo paid his countryman. Inside the building, a uniformed guard sat at a desk. Chiun approached him. "We look for Mr. Forsythe."

"This is ridiculous," Remo said.

The guard said, "Do you have an appointment? Is he expecting you?"

Chiun said, "The Master of Sinanju needs no appointment."

"The what?"

"Tell him that the Master of Sinanju and his servant are here," Chiun said.

"I'm the servant," said Remo.

"I am the Master of Sinanju," said Chiun.

"And I'm the white queen. Go away."

Chiun reasoned with the guard with a thumb in his clavicle and the guard realized it made great good sense to call Mr. Forsythe's office.

"Yes," he said into the phone with pain, "There's a man . . . a person here called the Master of Sinanju to see Mr. Forsythe. Ew-scray all-bay. Yes, I'll wait."

"What did that mean?" Chiun asked Remo.

"What?"

"What was that he said?"

"He said you were a screwball."

Chiun glared down at the guard who said into the phone, "Mr. Forsythe doesn't know any Master of Sinanju?" He looked up in helplessness. "Tell him Remo's here, too," suggested Remo.

"Someone named Remo's here, too," said the guard. "Please check." He waited a moment, then a smile relaxed his features. "Okay," he said and hung up the phone, gently because any quick movements hurt not just his shoulder but every muscle down to his waist. "He'll see you."

"Let go of him, Chiun," said Remo.

Chiun squeezed once hard, then released the guard who clapped his left hand to his right shoulder to try to massage away the pain.

"There is no hope for a country in which the name of Remo is a passport while the name of the Master goes unknown," Chiun said.

"You know how us whites are," said Remo. "Thick as thieves."

"Hear, hear," said Chiun with an evil cackle. "Hear, hear."

Forsythe awaited them in his office on the fifth floor of the building. He remained seated behind his desk in a large infield-sized room as Chiun and Remo entered and Remo forgave the lack of manners as a sacrifice made to good taste because while seated, only Forsythe's shirt could be seen and it was pink with purple flowers, but later when he stood, Remo saw he was wearing matching pants which made him look like a Bahamian shell peddler. He needed a straw hat to

120

complete the getup, decided Remo, who later saw a straw hat on a table in the corner.

"Good to see you again, Mister Master," Forsythe said to Chiun. "And you too, what is it, Remo?"

And Remo knew that Forsythe knew very well what it was and that it was Remo and that it was Remo's head that Mr. Gordons wanted or else he would paper an entire city with bogus money.

Chiun nodded. Remo did nothing.

"What can I do for you?" asked Forsythe. Remo looked at Chiun, who stood motionless in front of Forsythe's desk, saying nothing.

To fill the vacuum of silence, Remo said, "We wondered how you were doing with Mr. Gordons."

Forsythe lied. "Oh, we're still trying to track him down. After you got those plates from him at the airport, we haven't heard anything from him. Nothing at all. Have you had any luck?"

One good lie deserved another. "We did a little research into his background," Remo said. Chiun shot him a warning glance. Remo blithely went on. "He's from a small town in Missouri. His father, now dead, was a printer. His mother took in washing. He went to local schools, somehow avoided service in Korea, and was a schoolteacher. His hobbies are making models, watching baseball games on television, and needlepoint. He does not drink or smoke but is a member of no organized church."

"That's very good," Forsythe said with enthusiasm. "It's really fine how you two have found out so much in such a short period of time. Impressed, fella. Really impressed I am."

Remo smiled foolishly in response to Forsythe's foolish smile. Chiun continued staring at the man behind the desk.

"Maybe if we work together, fellas, we can get this Mr. Gordons," Forsythe said hopefully.

"Maybe, fella," Remo said. "Full speed ahead. We could really do it. Working together, both pulling one oar and all."

"Absolutely," said Forsythe. "Precisely my exact sentiments. You have a place to stay in town?"

Remo shook his head.

Forsythe said, "Just a minute," and picked up the phone. He dialed a number and asked for the manager. "Hello, Frederick. Forsythe here. Some very important people . . ." he winked at Remo ". . . have just come to town and I want you to put them up tonight. Some kind of a special room. Second floor. Near the center elevators. That sounds fine. Make the reservation in the name of Mister Master of . . . never mind, make it for Mr. Remo. See you, Frederick."

He hung up with a satisfied smile on his face. "That's the Carol Arms. He's saving room 226 for you. Nice digs, fellas. Why don't you get some sleep there and we'll talk tonight after you rest. I'll call you. Maybe we'll hear something from Mr. Gordons." He smiled hopefully at Remo. Chiun still stared at Forsythe.

Remo nodded.

Forsythe stood and Remo saw his flowered trousers. Forsythe reached forward a hand to Remo who shook it. He extended his hand toward Chiun but Chiun pretended not to see it, still staring into Forsythe's eyes. The proffered hand hung momentarily in the air, like a yo-yo at the top of its climb, before it dropped quickly to his side.

"Well, we'll talk tonight, fellas," said Forsythe. "It's really been good to see you. I'd been wondering if we would meet again. Kind of hoping we would. After our first meeting."

He sat down again, indicating the audience was over. Remo turned to the door. Chiun took a last look at Forsythe, then followed behind Remo. At the doorway, Remo glanced into a mirror on the wall. Forsythe's hand was already snaking out toward the telephone and he was drumming his fingers impatiently, waiting for them to leave before he picked up the instrument.

In front of the building, Remo said, "Quite the conversationalist, aren't you?"

"I have nothing to say to that man. He dresses funny."

"Didn't anybody every tell you it's not polite to stare? What were you looking at anyway?"

"I was looking at his head."

CHAPTER NINE

The room was a perfect setup. It was in the back of the hotel, near the elevator. The fire escape ran down alongside it to the alley, and the pull-down ladder could be grabbed from the ground by a jumping man. A squad of men could file up it to the platform outside room 226. With the door and the window covered, occupants would have no way to escape.

"It's a setup, Chiun," said Remo, looking around the room, kicking off his Italian loafers, and plopping backward onto the bed.

"Yes," said Chiun. His eyes were on the color television set. He went over and quickly turned the set on. "Do you know I have missed my beautiful stories for almost two weeks?"

"Heavens to Betsy," exclaimed Remo. "You see the way he looked at me?"

"Yes," said Chiun. "Like a dish for his palate."

The set slowly rearranged confusion into an image.

"Why'd you want to see him anyway?" asked Remo.

"We are attacking Mr. Gordons. We cannot be

distracted by this baboon in flowered pants coming after your head."

Remo grunted. "I wonder if Forsythe will come after us himself?"

Chiun began turning the channel selector, looking with only faint hope for one of his afternoon soap operas, even though the sun was sinking slowly in the west.

"He will come himself," he said.

"Why are you so sure?"

"Because your Mr. Forsythe is an idiot. Shhhh," said Chiun. He continued turning the dials but found only news programs and a science show for children. He slammed the on-off button of the set with a blow so vicious that it cracked the edge of the television case.

"This is a whole nation of idiots," he said. "Why should Mr. Forsythe be different from either you or the idiots who plan your television shows, those vile poll-takers of Washington. This is the headquarters of your government, isn't it?"

"Yes."

"Well, why is there nothing on television from your government? If they will not have the beautiful stories all the time, why do they not have your government shows on television? The last show they had was very good with the fat man asking questions and the Hawaiian who talked funny. I thought everybody liked that show. Why did they take it off?"

"It wasn't a show," Remo explained. "It was a Senate committee and when their work was done, they stopped."

"That wasn't a show?"

"No."

"That was your government in operation?"

"Yes."

"God help America."

Group Leader Francis Forsythe, on loan from the CIA to the Treasury Department, was not content to wait for God to help America, because, as Chiun had correctly discerned, he was an idiot.

As soon as Chiun and Remo had left his office, he called in the top aides he had brought with him from the CIA "to wrap up this little bogus money thing."

He sat, feet up on the desk, smoking a cigarette in a long water-impregnated filter-holder, and waited for the three staff men to assemble.

The last one to enter asked, "What's up, chief?"

"We're going to a beheading," Forsythe said, grinning.

He sat up quickly, stubbed his cigarette out in an ashtray, and rubbed his hands together in joyful anticipation of the coming night's activities. For this— overt activity—was what Forsythe knew he did best. It was how he had made his reputation and had begun his climb up through government ranks.

He had been a code officer in Europe during World War II when the Nazis set a trap for the American troops. An intelligence unit had intercepted a German code message. It was shipped by the commanding general to Forsythe who gave it to a clerk to decode. Five minutes later, the general called, demanding a deciphering. Forsythe yanked the message out of the clerk's hands, along with the partial translation, and headed for the general's tent.

He tried to finish the decoding as he walked. When he got to the tent, he told the general that the Germans were planning to capture two towns as part of a spearhead into American-controlled territory. The first town, Forsythe said, had been "hardly hit." That's what the German message said, he told the general.

The general rushed units to the first town. When they got there, they found that the Germans were in the second town and the Americans had sealed off their escape route.

The Nazis surrendered. Their commander wanted to know why the Americans hadn't fallen into the trap.

"What trap?" Forsythe asked him through an interpreter.

The Nazi officer explained that their coded message had been meant to be intercepted. "When you got it and it said the first town was hard hit, we expected your troops to come to the second town where we could trap them. Instead you went to the first town and got behind us. Why?"

"Superior planning," said Forsythe, who refused to believe that he had been too big a fool to be fooled.

His work with the code won him a major commendation and a promotion and led to his joining the CIA after the war. There had followed other successes, many of them equally accidental, and now, years later, he was behind a desk in the Treasury Building, trying to save America from a counterfeiting menace, but still yearning for the days when he fought and beat the Nazi menace almost single-handed.

Well, even if there were no more Nazis, there were still enemies. Mr. Gordons was one. And from what little he had been able to see, this anti-organization Remo person was probably another. And if one enemy wanted another enemy's head, well, then who was hurt?

True enough, this Remo had high clearance. But

no one need ever know that Forsythe had decided himself to deliver up Remo's head to Mr. Gordons— that is, until Forsythe was sure the act would draw credit instead of blame. For the time being, its justification was the need of the Republic.

Forsythe and his top aides carefully worked out their plans for the night. The Oriental was expendable. If he should get in the way, he would have to die too. But it was Remo's body—or at least a portion thereof —that they needed.

As he spoke, Forsythe's eyes glistened and nervously he ran a hand over his puffy cheeks, cheeks in which flesh had muted the outlines of what once had been high, hard cheekbones.

"Speed is important, but timing is even more important," said Forsythe. "The element of surprise is with us. They'll be sitting ducks. They're not expecting a thing. We'll rendezvous at 11:55 P.M. in the alley."

"Should we have duck?" asked Chiun.

"I hate duck," said Remo. "Besides they may not have time to cook it right before Forsythe attacks."

Chiun shook his head. "He will not attack before midnight."

"Why?"

"I have already explained that. He is an idiot. Idiots always attack at midnight."

This annoyed Remo, who had been lying on one of the beds trying to decide on the best time for a sneak attack and had settled on midnight.

"Oh, yeah?" said Remo.

"Should we have duck?" asked Chiun patiently.

"No. No duck." Remo snatched up the phone and told room service to send up rice and fish.

When dinner was over, Chiun suggested they go to

128

sleep. "We will probably have a hard day tomorrow."

Remo nodded as he took the two empty dinner plates. He balanced one of them atop the window leading into the room from the fire escape and slipped the other edge-first at eye level into the crack of the hotel room door.

Chiun watched him without comment.

"Sort of an early warning system," Remo explained. Chiun mumbled under his breath.

Later when the lights were out and all was still in the room, Remo felt a draft, a faint motion of breeze. But he heard nothing.

Then he heard Chiun's voice. "Plates. Why not cow bells? Or flares? Or hire guards to tell us when they are coming? Tricks. Always he wants to use tricks. Never does he understand that the essence of the art is purity."

Remo still could not see him and could hear only Chiun's voice as Chiun took the plate out of the door and the other from the window and placed them silently on a small end table.

Remo lay on the bed in silence, barely breathing.

Chiun, satisfied now that both he and Remo were properly defenseless, curled up onto his straw mat in the corner and fell asleep almost instantly. But before he did he said softly, "Good night, Remo, for you are still awake."

"How's a guy supposed to sleep with all that racket?" Remo asked.

The attack came at 12:00:48 A.M.

It was preceded by one of Forsythe's men kicking over one of the garbage cans in the alley below the fire escape. The aide then used the can to stand on to grab the fire escape ladder which unloosened and lowered with the squeak of a ship grinding against an iceberg.

Forsythe however did not hear this noise. After having synchronized watches with two of his men who had remembered to wear them, he took the third assistant, named Al, entered the hotel through a back door, and went up the back staircase to the second floor. Moving along the hallway toward room 226, Forsythe brushed against a table and upset a vase of plastic flowers.

Forsythe left it where it lay and then waited with Al outside room 226. He stood in silence, clenching and unclenching his hands, feeling the blood course through to his fingertips. The fingertips were the key. They would tell him when he was psychologically ready to move. He rubbed his fingertips against the heels of his hands.

Inside the room, Remo said softly, "Are you awake, Chiun?"

"No. I am going to sleep through my murder."

"Why are they waiting out there?" asked Remo.

"Who knows? They are probably stroking their fingertips."

Forsythe finished stroking his fingers, glanced at his watch, and slowly inserted the key into the lock, fumbling with it slightly because his eyes were on the luminous dial of his battery-operated Timex.

Behind him, Al shuffled nervously from foot to foot, his weight centered first over his right foot, then over his left, having found by sheer instinct the only way possible for a human being never ever to be balanced.

Finally, the sweep second hand of Forsythe's watch reached the eleven. Five seconds to go. He took a well-worn .32 caliber pistol, used for countless hours on a practice range, from inside his jacket, then turned the key, pushed open the door and jumped inside. His aide jumped in after him. Forsythe stopped short and

Al plowed into him, sending Forsythe stumbling a few steps more into the room. The room was illuminated now by the light from the hallway and Remo turned his head in Chiun's direction and shook his head in pity. Forsythe saw Remo in the bed, after recovering his balance, and sneered. He did not see Chiun, still curled up on his mat in the corner of the room.

Forsythe sneered again, waiting for his two assistants to come in the window, to trap his prey in a pincers movement.

There was silence in the room as everybody waited. Al stood by uncomfortably and wished that Forsythe had let him carry a gun. But Forsythe had insisted that the only gun on the mission be his.

They kept waiting. Finally, thirty-three seconds later by Remo's measure, there was a squeak at the window. All turned to look. The two agents were tugging mightily on the window from outside trying to raise it, but it was freshly painted and stuck fast.

"Oh, for God's sakes," said Forsythe.

"Listen, buddy," said Remo to Forsythe. "Is this almost a wrap?"

Remo's voice brought Forsythe back to his sense of duty and responsibility.

Satisfied that he no longer needed the men on the fire escape, he angrily waved them away. They leaned against the window, pressing their noses to the glass, looking in. Finally Forsythe raised both his hands over his head and waved them away, shouting, "Go home," unmistakably dismissing the two aides with wristwatches. They paused a moment. Remo could see them shrug, then they turned away from the window. A moment later there was the awesome screech of the ladder as it slid downward toward the ground. A minute later the screech was repeated as the men disembarked and the ladder started back up.

Forsythe watched until long after the window was empty.

"C'mon, c'mon, I don't have all night," Remo said.

"I suppose you want to know why you're going to die," Forsythe said, pulling his lips back to make them seem thin and sardonic.

"Sure would, old buddy," Remo said.

"Your death is required for the welfare of the United States of America."

"So that's what they mean by do and die," Remo said.

"Right," said Forsythe. Belatedly realizing that anyone walking down the hall might become suspicious if they looked through the open door and saw a man with a gun aimed at another man, he said over his shoulder to Al, "Turn on the light and close the door."

Al turned on the lamp on the table behind Forsythe and turned to walk toward the door.

"The door first," Forsythe said angrily. "Not the light first. The door first."

"Sorry about that, chief," said Al. He leaned back to the lamp and turned it off, then went in the darkness to close the door, planning to come back next and turn on the lamp again.

Forsythe sipped air in disgust. In the moment when both men were blinded by the flash of the lamp light, Chiun rose from his mat in the corner of the room and moved toward the door. When Al reached it, Chiun pushed him outside and hissed, "Go home. You are not needed," and closed the door, all in one fluid movement.

Al found himself on the outside of a locked door.

He could not get back in without knocking. But if he knocked, the chief might be distracted and lose his control of the situation. He had better just wait quietly, Al decided.

In blackness now, with the door closed, Chiun moved behind the unseeing Forsythe and turned on the lamp.

"Good, Al," Forsythe said. "Now you got it right." He looked at Remo. "The old Chinaman's not with you tonight, I see."

"Oh, sure he is."

"Don't lie to me, fella. His bed's not been slept in."

"He sleeps on the floor in the corner," said Remo.

Forsythe followed Remo's arm to the corner and saw Chiun's mat there.

He nodded. "Went out, huh?"

"No," said Remo.

"Where is he?"

"Right behind you."

Without turning around, and smirking at Remo for trying such an old trick, Forsythe said over his shoulder, "Al, you see that old Chinaman?"

Al, out in the hallway, could not hear Forsythe, so he did not answer.

"Al, dammit, I'm talking to you," said Forsythe.

"Mister Al is not here," said Chiun.

Jumping forward as if jolted by electricity, Forsythe hopped ahead, spun, and saw Chiun. He backed away toward the window, so he would be out of the lunging reach of the two men and could still cover both of them at the same time.

"Oh, it's you," he said.

Chiun nodded. "I am always me."

"I hope I won't have to kill you, old timer," said Forsythe, "but I will if you move a muscle. Without even a second thought, I'll blow you to smithereens."

"Careful, Chiun," said Remo. "He's a cold-blooded killer."

Forsythe turned back toward Remo. "I was about to tell you why you're going to die."

"Let's get on with it," Remo said. "I want to get some sleep."

"You're going to take that big sleep," Forsythe said.

"Good," said Remo.

"But first I have to tell you why you must die. I owe it to you." Remo looked at Chiun in hopeless supplication. Chiun sat down on the edge of the lamp table. He would not stand forever, even if this fool insisted on talking forever.

Forsythe went ahead to tell Remo that Remo's life was the price Mr. Gordons demanded to stop undermining America's economy. "I'm here to pay that price," he said. He explained that his normal position on ransom was not to pay it, but that these were extraordinary circumstances. "I have to face my responsibilities. I hope you'll face your responsibilities as a government man too and go quietly and willingly. It's bigger than both of us. I'm sure you'll agree." He paused for an answer. The only sound in the room was the faint hiss of breath from the sleeping Remo's nostrils.

Forsythe looked at Chiun. "How can you kill a man who isn't conscious?" he asked.

"It is easy," said Chiun. His right hand, resting on the edge of the table, had grasped one of the dinner plates he had put their earlier. Holding the edge between thumb, index, and middle fingers, he brought his arm forward fluidly, smoothly. The plate seemed glued to the end of his fingertips as his arm moved in Forsythe's direction. At the last moment, when it seemed the plate must surely drop to the floor, his wrist snapped with an audible crack and the plate flew toward Forsythe with a speed that made it invisible.

It rotated so fast it whirred, but the whirring lasted only a split second before it was succeeded by a buzzing thunk as the dull leading edge of the plate hit into, spun against and sawed, and then slipped through Forsythe's neck. The plate, pinkened with a slick of blood, clunked off Forsythe's left shoulder and dropped to the floor.

Forsythe's eyes were still wide open, his mouth still twisted in the expression of the last word he was about to say, then his body, no longer held upright by life, crumpled toward the floor, dropping out from under Forsythe's no-longer-attached head, which dropped down a split second later, hitting the back of the corpse and rolling toward the wall.

Remo slept on.

Chiun went to the door and opened it. Al was pacing nervously back and forth in front of the door.

"Your employer says to go home," said Chiun. "He is going to stay."

"Is everything all right?"

"Go home," said Chiun and closed the door.

Back in the room, he went to Forsythe's head and grasped it by its dark brown hair and looked at the features. Fatty but close enough. Using the edge of his hand, first as an ax then as a scalpel, Chiun began to attack the head, battering it and molding it, so that it would no longer be recognizably Forsythe, so that it would no longer be definitely not Remo.

It took thirty seconds. When Chiun was done, Forsythe's nose had been broken so that it looked as if it might have once been Remo's nose. Extra flesh had been compressed off Forsythe's cheeks and jowls to resemble Remo's high, protruding cheekbones. The bones of the eye sockets were broken so Forsythe's eyes, in death, sagged deeper into the sockets resembling Remo's brooding, deep eyes.

The ears. The ears were not right, Chiun thought as he looked down at the bloody lump on the floor. He glanced toward the bed where Remo slept. Remo had almost no lobes at all. Forsythe had long full earlobes which Chiun decided was characteristic of Americans and rightfully so, since if they were all going to act like jackasses, they might as well share with them not just intellect but ears. With his hardened fingertips and nails, he began to shave the excess flesh away from Forsythe's earlobes. He leaned back to inspect. Still not right.

With two slashes of his right hand, he took off the excess flesh, rendering Forsythe lobeless. It might not be perfect, but it was the best he could do. It would have to do. He hoped it would do.

Chiun removed a plastic tablecloth from the lamp table and wrapped the head inside it tightly, then stuffed the whole lump into a pillowcase he ripped from one of the pillows on his bed. He put the pile onto the sofa and looked around the room. Forsythe's headless body still lay in the middle of the floor. That would not do. The whole point of the deception would be lost if Forsythe's headless body were found and the press reported it, as they reported all such trivia to this nation of trivia collectors.

Chiun went to the window leading to the fire escape. He hit the heels of both hands simultaneously against both sides of the window, then with his right index finger pushed upward. The window slid smoothly and

136

easily upward and Chiun leaned out to see the garbage pail down below the fire escape.

Easily, he hoisted Forsythe's body through the window and onto the fire escape. He removed the man's wallet from his pocket, then held the body over the edge of the fire escape and dropped it. It slid down into the garbage pail smoothly, not touching the side before the feet hit bottom, like spitting into a sink.

Chiun looked down satisfied. If there were one of those insidious newspaper articles, it would talk about the headless body found outside Mr. Remo's room. That was fine for what Chiun had in mind. He went to the bathroom and flushed Forsythe's wallet down the toilet. The gun on the floor was another problem. Using his hand as a knife, Chiun slashed open one of the couch cushions and stuffed the gun deep inside it.

Then he picked up the pillowcase bundle, took one last look at Remo sleeping, and left the room, locking the door behind him, lest burglars sneak in and disturb Remo's rest.

"Heh, heh, heh, old timer. Delivering your Christmas packages early this year?"

The airport guard chuckled as he addressed Chiun, who was wearing a red robe and carrying his pillowcase over his shoulder like Santa's sack.

"Do not labor yourself with attempts to be funny. Where is the Eastern Airlines resignation desk?"

"Resignation desk?"

"Where they write many copies of tickets because you need only one to get on a plane."

"Oh, the reservations desk. Heh, heh," the sallow-faced guard said. "Down there, old-timer." He waved toward the other end of the terminal's main passenger building.

Chiun wordlessly walked away from him.

He saw the litter basket in front of the Eastern Airlines desk.

And then his senses told him Mr. Gordons was near but he did not know why. He sensed people because people had a living pulse, a rhythm of their own. Machines vibrated. Mr. Gordons vibrated; Chiun had recognized only lately that they were not human vibrations. He felt those vibrations now. They grew stronger as he approached the trash basket.

Glancing around him cautiously to see that no one was watching, and satisfied that no one was, Chiun dropped the little white sack into the top of the basket.

The vibrations that were Mr. Gordons were so strong, they almost made Chiun's flesh quiver.

Wherever he was, he was watching Chiun now. Chiun made sure that his face showed only sorrow, the appropriate look for an old man surrendering his pupil's head, then turned and walked away from the basket, softly along the hard terminal floor, toward the door through which he had entered.

Twenty-five yards from the ticket counter, the vibrations had almost vanished. Chiun turned. He was just in time to see the back of Mr. Gordons, stiffly carrying the white pillowcase at his side, disappear through a revolving door at the other end of the terminal.

Chiun looked toward the Eastern Airlines reservation desk.

The litter basket was gone. Where it had stood, there was only a small pile of papers, pop cans, and cigarette butts on the floor. But the litter basket itself was gone, nowhere to be seen.

CHAPTER TEN

Back in the hotel room, Chiun awakened Remo from his sound sleep.

"Come, we must find different lodgings," he said.

"What happened to Forsythe?" asked Remo. He looked around the room and saw the ubiquitous blood stain. "Never mind," he said. "Where have you been? What have you been up to?"

"Just getting your head together," said Chiun with a high-humored cackle. He felt this so good, it deserved repeating. "Getting your head together. Heh, heh, heh, heh."

"Oh, knock it off," said Remo rolling out of bed. Once on his feet, he saw the blood-slicked plate in the corner of the room.

"I guess my plates came in handy," he said. "Aren't you glad I thought of them?"

"I've changed my mind," Chiun said.

"About what?"

"Nobody can get your head together. Heh, heh, heh, heh."

In a small room across the city, a room with not one piece of furniture, Mr. Gordons sat on the floor. He grasped the pillowcase package between his two hands and gently, with no sign of strain or exertion, pulled his hands apart. The pillowcase ripped and the plastic tablecloth inside pulled apart with little strands of fluff from its flannel back fluttering onto the floor.

Mr. Gordons dropped the two halves of the package binding and looked down at its grizzly, blood-soaked contents.

"Very good," he said aloud. Since he had reprogrammed himself with the elementary creativity program developed by Dr. Vanessa Carlton's laboratory, he had taken to speaking his thoughts aloud. He wondered why he did this, but he was not quite creative enough to figure out that five-year-olds spoke to themselves, not because it had anything directly to do with their creativity, but because their growing creativity made them for the first time realize that they were but specks in a giant, unfathomable world and that made them lonely.

These thoughts were still beyond Mr. Gordons, and not having them, he did not even know that it was possible for him to have them.

"Very good," he repeated, putting his two hands down and touching the face. The head certainly looked like Remo's head. And the old Oriental, high probability name of Chiun, had certainly looked unhappy. Unhappy was what one was supposed to look like when one lost one's friend or had to make him give up his life. He had been told about such friends; the ancient Greeks had had many of them. Mr. Gordons was not quite sure what friend meant but if a friend worried about your loss, then was it not logical that a friend might help you to survive? It was, he decided.

Very logical. It was also creative. Mr. Gordons was pleased with himself. See: he had already become more creative. Creativity was a means of survival and survival was the most important thing in the world. A friend would also be a help to survival. He would have to get a friend. But that would have to wait.

For now, he would have to look more closely at this head. From the electronic circuits that coursed through his man-like body he withdrew the image of high probability name Remo. There it was. High cheekbones. This head had such cheekbones. Dark brown eyes sunk deep into the head. Mr. Gordons reached out a hand and pried open an eyelid. These were dark brown eyes and they appeared deepset, although his finger could tell that the bones were broken around the eye sockets and it was difficult to be sure. Dark brown hair.

He ran his fingers over the pulpy face of the severed head on the floor between his legs and worked out a correlation between his tactile impressions and the picture analysis of Remo he held in his head. There was no difference. Every dimension his fingers felt were the same dimensions his mechanical brain had measured in those times that he had seen high probability Remo.

Mr. Gordons slid his fingertips off the cheeks to the ears. The ears were badly mangled. Remo must have waged a gigantic struggle not to die. Perhaps he had fought with the old yellow-skinned man, high probability name Chiun. Mr. Gordons felt a desire to have seen that battle. That would have been worth seeing.

When first they had met, Remo had damaged Mr. Gordons. Mr. Gordons had thought for a time that Remo too might be an android. But no longer did he feel that way. After all, here was his head between

141

his feet, the one eye that had been pried open staring up at Mr. Gordons blankly, unseeing. The other eye remained tightly closed.

Mr. Gordons felt where the earlobes would have been.

The ears were twisted, cut, and bloodied. Why should ears be cut like that? The blow to the nose would kill a human. The blows that broke the eye socket bones would kill a human. The blows to the earlobes would not kill a human. They were mutilating wounds. Would the old man who looked sad have mutilated the head of high probability Remo? No. They were friends. He would someday have his own friend, thought Mr. Gordons. Would he mutilate the ears of his friend? No. Perhaps someone else had mutilated the head of Remo. Mr. Gordons thought about this for a moment. No. No one else could mutilate Remo. No one else but the aged yellow person could have killed him.

Why the mutilation?

Mr. Gordons brought all his creativity to bear upon the problem. He could not think of an answer. There must be danger in it. Danger to Mr. Gordons's survival. He must think about this more. More investigation. More data. More creativity.

He reached a pair of fingers into the matted flesh on the underside of the right ear. He felt something that did not belong there. It was of the wrong weight and mass and density. He extracted it. It was a small piece of skin. He felt it between his fingertips. It felt like the skin from the rest of the head. He held it close to his eye sensors and counted the pores per square millimeter on the small piece of skin, then lowered his head and made a random check of the number of pores per millimeter at three different

142

locations on the head. All were within chance tolerances. High probability, the piece of skin was from the ear of the dead person's head between his legs.

He carefully checked the ear to see where the piece of skin had been detached. He saw a little V-shaped cutout in the ear from which the skin had been removed. The pointed end of the scrap of skin in his hand fit into the V exactly. He held it in place with his left hand and extended the skin, down under and around the flesh to try to find where at the back of the ear the skin fit. He found it and held it there with his other hand. The piece of skin formed a U-shaped loop, but the loop was not fully filled with flesh from the ear. There was a space. Three and a half millimeters of space. The ear had been made smaller. Some of the flesh had been removed. He looked again at the loop of skin, correctly anchored in front of and in back of the ear. If that skin had been filled with flesh, as in life it had, that much flesh would have created an earlobe. But high probability Remo had no earlobes.

Therefore this was not the head of high probability Remo.

It was logical. He was correct. While he had no instincts to sense correctness, he knew he was right because his sensory apparatus was infallible.

He left the head on the floor and stood up, looking down at it.

It was not Remo's head. As he looked at it again, he tried to decide whose head it might be, but he did not know. Never mind; he knew it was not Remo's.

The old yellow-skin had tried to deceive him. He had said that he would not challenge Mr. Gordons's survival but now he was doing that by trying to deceive Mr. Gordons. Now he too must die. High probability Chiun must die along with high probability Remo. Mr. Gordons would see to that.

But there were other things he must do. He must drop money on a city as he said he would.

And he must find a friend.

CHAPTER ELEVEN

"If you will be my friend, I will give you a drink. Will you be my friend?"

The pilot of the Pan Am jet looked with amusement at the ordinary-looking man standing in front of him, holding a large cardboard carton in his arms.

Captain Fred Barnswell had a date. The new stew on his flight had made it very clear that she had the hots for him and he had just finished filing his flight reports and was on his way to his Manhattan apartment where she would be joining him for a late dinner.

He had no time for aviation groupies, particularly middle-aged male variety.

"Sure, buddy, sure. Whatever you want. I'll be your friend for life."

The ordinary-looking man smiled with gratitude but he did not move. He still stood in Captain Barnswell's way in the narrow corridor leading from the pilots' offices toward the main terminal at Kennedy Airport outside New York City.

"Okay, buddy?" said Barnswell with a smile. He

was in a horny hurry. "Now what do you say, you move along."

"Good," said the man. "Now that you are my friend, you will do a favor for me, correct?"

Here it comes, thought Barnswell. Another bum putting the bite on. Why him all the time? He must have a kind face.

"Sure, buddy," he said reaching into his pocket. "Now much do you need? Quarter? Buck?"

"I need your aircraft."

"What?" said Barnswell, wondering if perhaps he should call airport security right away.

"Your aircraft. It is not too much for a friend to ask."

"Look, buddy, I don't know what your game is, but . . ."

"You will not give me your aircraft?" The smile vanished from the man's face. "Then you are not my friend. A friend would care about my survival."

"All right, enough's enough. Why don't you get out of here before you get into trouble?"

"Is there another pilot here who will be my friend and who will lend me his aircraft?"

I don't know why I bother, thought Barnswell. Maybe I *am* kind. Patiently he said, "Look, friend, the planes don't belong to us. They belong to the airlines. We just work for the company. I can't lend you my plane because I don't own a plane."

The smile returned to the man's face. "Then you really are my friend?"

"Yes," said Barnswell.

"Does no one have his own aircraft?"

"Only private pilots. The small planes you see. They're privately owned."

146

"Will one of them be my friend? Can a person have more than one friend at a time?"

"Sure. All of them will be your friends. Pick any six." What a story Barnswell would have to tell that stew while he was getting her drawers down.

"You are a real friend," said the man, still smiling. "Have a million dollars. See, I will be your friend, too." He put down the cardboard carton and opened the top. It was filled to the brim with hundred-dollar bills. There must be millions in the box, thought Barnswell. Maybe billions. It had to be fake. There wasn't that much cash on hand in a bank, much less in a cardboard box being carried around by some brain-damage case.

"That's all right, buddy," said Barnswell. "I don't need your money to be your friend. Where'd you get all that anyway?"

"I made it."

"Made it like manufactured or made it like earned?"

"Like manufactured, friend," said the man.

"Well, buddy, I think you ought to turn it over to the authorities."

"Why, friend?" asked the smiling man.

"Because it'll go easier with you if you turn yourself in. The government just doesn't like people printing money on their own."

"They will arrest me?"

"Maybe not right off, but they would want to question you."

"And you say I should do this?" asked the smiling man.

"Sure should, pal. Come clean. 'Fess up."

"You are not a true friend," said the smiling-faced man who was suddenly no longer smiling. He swung his right arm through the air and where the side of his

147

hand struck Captain Barnswell's head, the temple bones shattered and Captain Barnswell left instantly for that big stewardess hutch in the sky.

Mr. Gordons looked down at the body with no feeling but puzzlement. Where had their friendship gone wrong?

The next man he met was small and wiry with bad teeth and a faded blue pilot's cap with a fifty-mission crush. He owned an old DC-4 and he was delighted to be Mr. Gordons's friend and he did not suggest that Mr. Gordons turn his money over to the authorities, this most especially after satisfying himself that the box was really full of money, and if it was counterfeit —and he had had some experience in moving fake money—it was the best counterfeit he had ever seen.

Sure he would be glad to take Mr. Gordons for a plane ride. Anything for a friend. Cash in advance. Two thousand dollars.

Airborne, Mr. Gordons asked him where the place of greatest population density was.

"Harlem," said the pilot. "The jungle bunnies there are like rabbits. Everytime you turn around, they've bred another one."

"No," said Mr. Gordons. "I mean dense with people, not with bunnies or rabbits. I am sorry I do not make myself so clear."

"You're clear enough, pal," said the pilot to Mr. Gordons, sitting in the co-pilot's seat next to him. "Next stop, 125th Street and Lenox Avenue."

When they were homing in over Harlem, the pilot asked Mr. Gordons why he wanted to see such a dense area from the sky.

"Because I want to give my money away to the people there."

"You can't do that," the pilot said.

148

"Why not can I?"

"Because those blooches'll just buy more Cadillacs and green shoes with it. Don't waste your dough."

"I must. I promised. Please, friend, fly low over this Harlem rabbit preserve."

"Sure, buddy," said the pilot. He watched as Mr. Gordons lifted the box and went to the right fuselage door of the quarter-century-old plane. If that looney-toon was going to open the door, well, maybe it wouldn't be money dropping on Harlem but looney-toon himself.

Mr. Gordons slid back the door of the plane. The pilot felt the whoosh of wind circulating through the aircraft. He turned the plane slightly to the right, then banked sharply to the left, throwing it into full throttle. The inertial straight-line motion of his body should have thrown Mr. Gordons out of the open door.

Nothing happened. He merely stood there, poised on his two feet in the open doorway. He had the cardboard box jammed up against the plane wall near his feet and he reached in and began to grab handfuls of money and to throw it through the open door. As the pilot watched over his shoulder, the money sucked in alongside the plane, caught in its air currents, then slowly drifted loose and began to float down onto pre-dawn Harlem.

The pilot again tried the right turn and left bank in the hope of dislodging Mr. Gordons. It failed again and the early morning money distribution continued.

Five more times he tried and each time Mr. Gordons just stood there as if nothing had happened and kept throwing out money. Finally, the money box was empty.

Mr. Gordons left the door open and walked back to the cockpit. The pilot looked at him in awe.

"How much did you toss out there?"

"One billion dollars," said Mr. Gordons.

"Hope you saved some for me, old buddy," the pilot said.

"You are not my buddy and I am not yours. You tried to damage me by making me fall from the plane. You are not my friend."

"But I am, I am, I am your friend." The pilot kept screaming this as he was dragged from his seat, along the aisleway to the open door. "You can't fly this craft," he shouted. "You'll crash," he called as he went through the open door and plummeted, un-moneylike, decisively, straight for the ground. The plane took a slight dip forward and Mr. Gordons went back and sat in the pilot's seat. Why was piloting supposed to be difficult? It was all very easy and mechanical. He made it seem that way as he took the plane back to Kennedy Airport. He knew nothing, however, of flight patterns so he ignored the chattering radio and just landed without clearance on the main east-west runway and taxied toward one of the terminals. He was barely missed by a landing Jumbo Jet which whooshed by him with a rush of air that almost made his own plane unmanageable. Mr. Gordons heard the radio squawk: "What the christ is going on in that DC-4? Herman, I'll have your goddamn license for this."

Mr. Gordons realized he had done something wrong and the authorities would be after him. He watched the first men moving toward the parked plane. They were policemen of some kind, wearing blue uniforms, peaked caps, and badges. He committed it to his mind so his fabricators would work more accurately. He looked over his shoulder. The passenger seats in the plane, the few that were left after the plane had been emptied for cargo carrying, were of a rough blue nubby material.

When the three policemen boarded his plane, they found no one there. They searched the plane carefully, even looking under the passenger seats whose fabric was ripped and torn. Later they were joined by more men, these in suits, and they never seemed to notice that the three uniformed police officers had become four uniformed police officers. And minutes later, Mr. Gordons, having restructured his uniform into a blue business suit, was walking through the main entrance of the terminal.

He would have to write another letter, demanding now not only the head of high probability Remo but the head of high probability Chiun. He might not survive in America if the two of them lived. He must devise a threat powerful enough so that the government would obey him. It would take all his creativity.

It was good. It would take his computers away from the nagging question of what had happened to his friendship. Perhaps some people were just destined not to have friends.

CHAPTER TWELVE

"It didn't work, Chiun," said Remo holding a copy of the late afternoon paper.

Emblazoned across the front page was a giant end-of-the-world typeface headline:

MONEY
COMES
TO
HARLEM

The story told how the streets had been blanketed with money during the night. It was accompanied by a photograph of some of the bills. When their photographer had gotten to Harlem all the money was off the streets, but he had stopped in a liquor store and there was able to photograph many bills. Two bank managers in the area were shown samples of the money and certified it as genuine.

The newspaper implied that there was some insidious plot behind throwing a billion dollars—that was their inspired guess—onto Harlem's streets, some kind of trick by the power structure to keep the struggling blacks in their place.

That the newspaper had the story at all was a tribute to the skills and persistence of some of the editorial staff.

Two hours after they learned that "something was up" in Harlem, they finally found out about the money. During those two hours, the staff had been working on a blockbuster story telling how Harlem had gone on strike, no one was reporting for work, and while there had been no announcements, the action was obviously well-organized and clearly a massive protest by the black community against bias, discrimination, and all forms of tokenistic, non-Jewish liberalism. When the money explanation was found, the editor took all the work that had been done on the "general strike" and put it in his top desk drawer. Plenty of time to use that another day.

The Treasury Department, asked about the money, would say only that it was investigating.

"We attack," said Chiun.

"But I thought this was going to work," needled Remo. "I thought he was going to think it was my head."

"He probably opened it and when he saw something inside the skull realized it could not be yours. We attack."

They spoke in a cab and moments later were aboard a plane to Dr. Carlton's labatories in Cheyenne, Wyoming.

The next day, Dr. Harold W. Smith at Folcroft Sanitarium had two disturbing items on his desk.

The first was an immaculately typed letter that looked like printing. It had come from Mr. Gordons to the Federal Bureau of Investigation, where it had been routed directly to the director's desk, and routed by him to the President's office, and had finally wound up on this most top secret desk of all. It said simply that unless Mr. Gordons was given the heads of Chiun and Remo, he would buy an entire Strategic Air Command group, by paying a million dollars to each of its members, and would use the equipment to blow up a number of American cities.

The second item was a newspaper clipping. It reported that Dr. Vanessa Carlton, head of the famous Wilkins Laboratory for space components and equipment, had announced that her staff had developed an entirely new creativity program. It would allow spacecraft computers to think originally for the first time in their history.

"Our earlier effort at a creativity program compares to this one as an imbecile compares to a genius," Dr. Carlton said. "With this program in operation, a spacecraft will be able to react brilliantly to any kind of unforeseen occurrence in space."

Dr. Carlton also announced that the equipment would be installed aboard a laboratory rocket and launched into space in two days.

Remo and Chiun had not reported in. They were alive. Smith knew that because Mr. Gordons had gone ahead with his threat and had dumped a billion dollars onto Harlem. But they had probably tangled with Mr. Gordons somehow. Why else would Mr. Gordons now raise his demand to include Chiun's head as well as Remo's?

Smith spun in his office seat and looked through the one-way glass toward the waters of Long Island Sound, lapping gently at the shoreline of Rye, New York. He had sat in that seat for more than ten years. Ten years with CURE. For Remo and Chiun, it had been the same. They were, along with Smith, indispensable parts of the operation.

A slight scowl crossed his pinched, sour-looking face and he raised his right hand to stroke his neatly shaved jaw. Indispensable? Remo and Chiun indispensable? Although alone in his office, he shook his head. There was no one who was indispensable. Not Remo, not Chiun, not Dr. Smith himself. Only America and its safety and its security was indispensable. Not even the President himself, the only other man who knew about CURE, was indispensable. Presidents came and Presidents went. The only thing indispensable was the nation itself.

But this latest note from Mr. Gordons had shaken him. It was Smith's responsibility to let the President know what his options were and this was a new President. Who knew what his response might be? Suppose he said simply, pay Mr. Gordons his price. That would be wrong, because blackmail always led to more blackmail and there was never an end to it. They should all fight. They should.

But years in government service had taught Dr. Smith that there was often a void between "should" and "did." And if the President said to sacrifice Remo and Chiun, then Smith would have no alternative but to try to find a way to deliver their heads to Mr. Gordons.

So much for loyalty and duty. But what of friendship? Did it count for nothing? Smith looked at the waves gently rolling up on the rocky shoreline, and made his decision. Before he would hand up Remo and Chiun, he would go after Mr. Gordons himself. It had, he insisted to himself, nothing to do with friendship. It was just the right administrative thing to do. But he could not explain to himself why this administrative decision—not to hand up Remo and Chiun without a fight—filled him with pleasure when other administrative decisions never had before.

He turned back to his desk and looked again at the clipping of Dr. Carlton's announcement. A creativity program. That was what Mr. Gordons wanted. With a creativity program, he could be unstoppable. Why had such a thing been announced? Didn't Dr. Carlton, who had created Mr. Gordons, know that such an announcement would bring Gordons running to her door to steal the program?

He read the clipping again. Words jumped from the paper at him. Creativity. Imbecile. Genius. Survival. And then he had a suspicion.

He picked up the telephone and set a program in motion that within minutes delivered to his desk the name of every passenger who had that day made a reservation to fly to Wyoming. What name might Mr. Gordons use? He was programmed for survival; he would not use his own. Humans taking aliases generally kept their initials; that was the extent of their creativity. Would Mr. Gordons? Smith look down the slim list of seventy names headed for the Cheyenne area that day. His finger stopped near the bottom of the list. Mr. G. Andrew. He knew. He knew. He didn't think, he knew without thinking, that that was Mr. Gordons. He had used his only initial and his description. He had changed android to Andrew. That was it.

Smith called his secretary and got a seat on the next plane to Wyoming. The launch was scheduled for tomorrow morning. Mr. Gordons would be there. He suspected that Remo and Chiun already were there.

And now so would Dr. Harold W. Smith.

CHAPTER THIRTEEN

The idea to use Dr. Carlton as a lure for Mr. Gordons had been Chiun's.

"A man must be attacked through what he perceives as his need," Chiun had explained to Remo.

"But Gordons isn't a man."

"Silence," said Chiun. "How do you learn anything? Everything feels need. Do you build a dam to stop a river in the desert where there is only flat land and the river will just curl around your dam? No, you build a dam where the river feels a need to run between mountains. Everything feels need. Do you understand?"

Remo nodded glumly. If he agreed quickly, he might be able to head off one of Chiun's unending stories about the thieving Chinese.

"Many years ago," Chiun said, "the thieving Chinese had an emperor who, even for such a people, was of a low order. And he did hire the Master of Sinanju to perform a minor service for him and then did refuse to pay him. He did this because he thought, with the arrogance of all Chinese, that he was above all rules.

157

He was, he said, a sun emperor and must be worshipped like the sun."

"So your ancestor punched his trip ticket," said Remo.

"That is not the point of this story," said Chiun. "This emperor did live in a castle surrounded by walls and guards and many devices designed to protect the emperor."

"Child's play to your ancestor," said Remo.

"Perhaps. But the village depended upon my ancestor for sustenance and therefore he could not risk his person. What did he do then, this ancestor? Did he go home to Sinanju and say 'Oh, I have failed. Send the babies home to the sea.' Because that is what they did with babies in Sinanju when there was starvation. They put them into the sea and they were 'sending them home' again but the people knew they were not sending them home but that they were really drowning them, because they could not feed them. Sinanju is, as you know, a very poor village and . . ."

"Chiun, please. I know all that."

"So this ancestor did not say, I have failed. He looked to see what the emperor's need was. Now this emperor could have stayed safe behind his walls for years. But he was vain and he thought the thieving Chinese could not govern themselves if he remained behind castle walls. He needed to feel important. And soon the emperor opened the gates of his palace so the people could come to him pleading for justice and mercy.

"And so my ancestor dirtied his face and borrowed a torn old robe . . ."

"Without paying for it, I bet," said Remo.

"He returned it; one need not pay when one returns a thing. And he did enter the palace in the guise

158

of a beggar and when the emperor, fat and complacent, was wallowing on his throne and satisfying what he felt was his need to rule, my ancestor did grab him by the throat and say I have come for my payment."

"Exit one emperor," said Remo.

"No," said Chiun. "The emperor paid him on the spot with many jewels and great amounts of coins that were of gold. And the people of the village were fed and the babies did not have to be sent home to the sea."

"And all because of what the emperor thought he needed?"

"Correct," said Chiun.

"Good for your ancestor. Now what has this got to do with Mr. Gordons?"

"He thinks he needs creativity to survive. If we tell him where he can get it, he will go there. And then we will attack."

"And this will work?"

"You have the promise of a Master of Sinanju."

"Hear, hear," said Remo. "I still think you should have let me go after him, head to head, me and him."

"See. You have a need, too," said Chiun. "You need to be stupid."

And then he would say no more until they stood before Dr. Carlton in her office at the Wilkins Laboratory. She was happy to see them.

"I've thought of nothing but you, Browneyes, since you left," she told Remo. "You've got a hell of a nerve. It took me three days to fix Mr. Jack Daniels. You really did a number on his transistors. On mine, too."

"Aw, shucks," said Remo. "Twere nothin'."

"Twere too something," she said, smoothing her

159

white nylon blouse down over her pillowy breasts. "You could take lessons from this man, Mr. Smirnoff," she called over Remo's shoulder. "You're supposed to be a pleasure machine, and you're not a pimple on his butt."

Remo turned. The android, Mr. Smirnoff, stood silently in a corner of the room looking at them. Was he watching? Listening? Or was he just propped up, empty, turned off? As he looked, Remo saw Mr. Smirnoff nod his head, as if in agreement with Dr. Carlton. Then his eyes turned and locked on Remo's. Remo turned away.

"Yes, you're really something, Browneyes."

"Yes, yes, yes, yes," Chiun said, "but we are here on important business."

"I never discuss business without a drink. Mr. Seagrams!" The self-powered cart rolled through the door and obeyed her command for a double dry, very dry, martini. She took a long sip of it while the liquor dispenser rolled away.

"Now what's on your mind?"

"You're going to announce the discovery of a new creativity program," Remo said.

Dr. Carlton laughed. "And you're going to walk on the ceiling."

"You have to," Remo said. Chiun nodded. "We need it to lure Mr. Gordons here."

"And that's just why I'm not going to do it. I've got no control over Mr. Gordons anymore. I don't know what he's likely to do if he shows up here. I don't need that headache. Why do you think I changed all the security at the entrances? No thank you. No thank you. No thank you."

"You misunderstand me," Remo said. "We're not

160

asking you to announce the program. We're telling you to." Chiun nodded.

"That's a threat, I take it."

"You've got it."

"What have you got to threaten me with?"

"This," said Remo. "The government cut off the funds for this place. But you're still operating as merrily as ever. On what? With what? Two cents will get you four that it's Mr. Gordons's counterfeit money. The government takes a dim view of people, even scientists, who go around spreading funny money."

Dr. Carlton took another long sip from her drink, then sat at her desk. She started to answer, then stopped, took another sip of the martini, and finally said, "All right."

"No arguments?" asked Remo. "Just 'all right'?"

She nodded.

"What gave you the idea of programming Mr. Gordons for counterfeiting anyway?" Remo asked.

"You browneyed bastard," she said. "You were just guessing."

Remo shrugged.

"I didn't program him for counterfeiting," she said heatedly. "One day I had a staff meeting about our money problems. I said the government was destroying us. I think I said that if we had money, we'd survive. Money always means survival. Something like that."

She finished the drink with an angry swallow and bellowed again for Mr. Seagrams.

"Anyway, Mr. Gordons was in the room. He overheard. That night he left. The next day he sent me a pile of counterfeit money. To help me survive, the note said."

"And with perfect counterfeits, it was easy," Remo said.

"At first they weren't perfect." She paused while the liquor cart refilled her glass. "But I kept sending the bills back to him with suggestions. Finally he got them right."

"Well now, we're going to get him right. Tonight you announce a new creativity program. Announce that you're going to test it the day after tomorrow on a rocket launch from here."

"I'll do it," Dr. Carlton said. "But what chance do you think you're going to have against him? He's indestructible. He's a survivor."

"We'll think of something," Remo said.

But Remo had misgivings. In their room at the laboratory that night, he told Chiun, "It's not going to work, Chiun."

"Why?"

"Because Mr. Gordons will see through it. He's going to know it's a phony and we're behind it. It doesn't take the creativity of a snail to see that."

"Aha," Chiun said, raising his long-nailed right index finger skyward. "I have thought of that. I have thought of everything."

"Why don't you tell me about it?"

"I will." Chiun opened his kimono at the throat. "Do you notice anything?"

"Your neck seems thinner. Have you been losing weight?"

"No, not my weight. Remember the lead lump I have been wearing about my neck? It is gone."

"Good. It was ugly anyway."

Chiun shook his head. Remo was dumb sometimes. "That was a thing from Mr. Gordons. One of those beep-beeps your government is always using. An insect, I think you call them."

"A bug?"

"Yes. That is it. An insect. Anyway, I kept it and buried it in lead so Mr. Gordons would get no signals from it."

"So?"

"So when we came here, I took it out of the lead, so Mr. Gordons *would* get signals."

"Well, that's dumb, Chiun. Now he's going to know we're here. That's just what I said."

"No," Chiun said. "I put in it an envelope and mailed it away. To a place all Americans love and always go to."

"Where's that?"

"Niagara Falls. Mr. Gordons will see that we have gone away to Niagara Falls. He will not know we are here."

Remo raised his eyebrows. "It might work, Chiun. Very creative."

"Thank you. Now I am going to sleep."

Later, as Remo was drifting off to sleep, Chiun said, "Do not feel bad, Remo. You will be creative too one day. Maybe Dr. Carlton will make a program for you." And he cackled.

"Up yours," Remo said, but very quietly.

The next day, Dr. Carlton's announcement had appeared in the press. It came to the attention of two sets of eyes: the brilliant eyes of Dr. Harold W. Smith and the electronic sensors that reposed behind the plastic face of Mr. Gordons. Both had boarded planes for Cheyenne, Wyoming.

CHAPTER FOURTEEN

It was late the next day when Dr. Harold W. Smith presented himself at the steel gate outside the Wilkins Laboratories.

Remo was in the office with Dr. Carlton when she demanded to know who was at the door.

"Dr. Harold W. Smith," came back the voice.

Remo took the microphone from Dr. Carlton.

"Sorry. We have all the brushes we need," he said.

"Remo? Is that you?"

"Who's Remo?" asked Remo.

"Remo. Open this gate."

"Go away."

"Let me talk to someone in possession of all his faculties," insisted Smith.

Remo handed the microphone back to Dr. Carlton. "He must want to talk to you."

"Do you think I've got all my faculties?" she asked.

"You've got all of everything," Remo said.

"You really think so?"

"I've always thought so."

"What are you going to do about it?" Dr. Carlton asked.

"I know what I'd like to do."

"Yes?"

"But."

"But what?"

"But I don't really feel like making love to you *and* that computer too."

"Screw the computer," Dr. Carlton said.

"It'll have to wait its turn," said Remo.

"Remo, Remo," squawked Dr. Smith's voice.

Remo picked up the microphone. "Wait there a few minutes, Smitty. We're busy now."

"All right, but don't take forever."

"Don't tell him what to do," Dr. Carlton said into the microphone. She turned it off and said to Remo, "I don't like Dr. Smith."

"To know him is to dislike him. To know him well is to detest him."

"Let him wait."

Dr. Smith waited forty-five minutes before the steel panel opened. He walked along the corridor and the steel wall opened and he entered to find Remo and Dr. Carlton sitting at her desk.

"I knew you'd be here," he told Remo. "You're Dr. Carlton?"

"Yes. Dr. Smith, I presume?"

"Yes." He looked through the open doorway to the three-story-high control panel of the computer center. "That is quite something," he said.

"Mr. Daniels," she said. "Jack Daniels. There's nothing like it in the world."

"How many synapses?" asked Smith.

"Two billion," she said.

"Incredible."

"Come, I'll show you," and she rose to her feet.

Remo waited but was finally disgusted by so many "incredibles" and "marvelouses" and "wonderfuls" that he went back to his room, where Smith joined him and Chiun later and reported on Mr. Gordons's latest demand.

"Well, don't worry about it," Remo said. "He'll be here."

"I think he is here," Smith said. "There was a passenger booked on an earlier flight. Mr. G. Andrew. I think it was him."

"Then we'll see him in the morning."

Smith nodded and then said nothing more until he left for his room to sleep.

"The emperor is disturbed," said Chiun.

"I know it. He thinks this and he thinks that. When did you ever hear Smith anything less than positive?"

"He is worried about you," said Chiun. "He is afraid his emperor may tell him to hand up your head."

"My head? What about yours?"

"If it comes to that, Remo, you must tell Mr. Gordons that I am the sole support of a large village. It is different with you. You are an orphan and nobody relies on you. But many people will starve and want for food and shelter if I am no longer here to provide them."

"I'll try to put a good word in for you," Remo said.

"Thank you," said Chiun. "It is only right. After all, I am important. And creative."

Smith was in better spirits the next morning when he and Remo went to inspect the rocket launching chute. It was a giant brick tube, coated with steel plates, built into the center of the building. It stood as high as the top of the three-story building and

166

extended two stories below ground, fifty feet high in all.

A rocket sat in there now, a thirty-foot-high needle-shaped missile. Liquid oxygen was being poured into its motors by elaborate pumping equipment built into the walls. Looking into the chute, raised a few feet above the launch pad, was the control room, shielded behind a thick clear plastic window. A steel door was cut into the wall of the chute next to the window and led into the control room.

Inside the control room, Smith looked out at the rocket and asked Remo, "Is there a way we could lure him onto the rocket and launch him into space?"

Remo shook his head. "You don't understand. He's a survival machine. He'd figure a way to get back down. We've got to destroy the matter that he is created from. That's the only way to get him."

"Out of the way, boys." Dr. Carlton, all business in a long white robe, brushed by them and went to the control panel where she began flipping toggle switches and checking readings on the rocket's internal pressure. Walking along behind her was Chiun, who stood at her shoulder and watched her work.

"And you have a plan to accomplish this?" Smith asked Remo.

"Ask Chiun," Remo said. "He's creative."

Smith called Chiun over and asked, "Do you have a plan for destroying Mr. Gordons?"

"A plan is not required," said Chiun, turning around to watch Dr. Carlton at work. "He will come when he will come and when he comes I will attack him through his need. There will be no difficulty. She is a very nice woman."

"Are you jilting Barbra Streisand?" Remo asked. "After being in love with her for so long?"

167

"It is possible for one to love many," Chiun said. "After all, I am but one and I am loved by many. Should not the opposite be possible?"

"Will you two stop?" Smith said. "We can't just leave everything to chance. We've got to have a plan."

"Well, you go ahead and make one up," Remo said. "It's three hours to launch time. I'm going to have breakfast." He turned and walked away.

"Yes. You make up a plan," Chiun said to Smith and he walked away to stand again at Dr. Carlton's shoulder. "You move those switches nicely," he said.

"Thank you."

"You are an exceptional woman."

"Thank you."

Smith shook his head in exasperation, found a chair in the corner, and sat down to try to work out a plan. Somebody here should act sane.

At that moment, Mr. Gordons was acting very sane. He had walked up to the front door of the laboratory and read a sign which said that because of a rocket launching at noon, all personnel were given the day off.

Noon. His time sensors told him there were 172 minutes left till noon. He would wait. There would be no danger. The two humans, Remo and Chiun, were not here. The homing device showed they were someplace in the northeastern part of the United States. He would wait until it was nearer launch time. Optimum time when launching personnel would be busy with their tasks.

The clock over the plastic window behind the control board read 11:45.

Dr. Carlton sat at the panel, Smith at her side. She checked gauges continuously.

168

"It's all set," she called over her shoulder. "It can go anytime."

"Good," said Remo who was lying on a table. "Keep me posted."

Chiun stood by Remo's side.

"Hark," he said to Remo.

"What hark?"

"Did you not hear that sound?"

"No."

But Chiun had. He continued to listen for another sound like the first. He had recognized the first. It was the sound of metal being ripped. The steel door to the lab complex had been pulled open. A flashing red light came on over the control panel.

"He's here," Dr. Carlton said. Remo jumped to his feet and went to her side. "Someone's in the passageway," she said. "The heat sensor just came on."

"Good," said Remo. "Is there a way we can shade this window? So he can't see us?"

Dr. Carlton pressed a button. The clear plastic slowly began to darken. "There's a polaroid sheet in the center," she said. "By rotating it, you close out the light."

"Good," said Remo. "That's dark enough. Stop it now."

In the passageway that led to the rocket tube, Mr. Gordons moved slowly. There was ample time. Fourteen minutes left. A steel panel barred his way. He pressed his hands against the edge of the steel panel. His fingers lost their human shape as they turned into thin steel blades that slid into the opening between the panel and the wall. They extended until they reached the end of the panel, then curled around it. Mr. Gordons pulled. The panel groaned, surrendered, and flew open, revealing another corridor behind.

169

Mr. Gordons restructured his hands into human fingers as he walked. He reached the enclosed stairway at the end of the hall and walked up.

Three flights later, he was on the roof, walking toward the large opening in the center of the building that was the rocket shaft. He could see the droplets of liquid oxygen spurting over the edge. He reached the edge of the shaft and peered down. Below him he saw the sharp pointed nose of the rocket. A metal ladder curled over the edge and down into the pit, which fogged over with the fumes of the liquid oxygen. Mr. Gordons hoisted himself over and began climbing down the ladder.

"There he is," said Remo softly. "He still moves funny."

Mr. Gordons sensed humans behind the plastic screen but it did not bother him because there were supposed to be humans there. He reached the bottom of the rocket tube and walked until he stood in the liquid oxygen fog under the rocket.

"Cut that fog," Remo said to Dr. Carlton. "I can't see what he's doing."

Dr. Carlton pressed a button which cut off the supply of coolant to the rocket. As the mist began to dissipate, they saw Mr. Gordons reach over his head, grab the locked hatch of the rocket and wrench it off. He dropped it to his feet. He reached his hands over his head, grasping the two sides of the open hatch and hoisted himself up.

Smith's hand began to move toward the launch button but Remo clapped his hand over Smith's. "None of that," he said. "I told you it won't work."

"What will?"

"This."

Remo opened the door from the control room into

the rocket shaft and leaped lightly down to the floor of the tube. He heard above him, inside the rocket, the ripping tear of metal and machinery.

"Hey, you refugee from Oz, get down out of there," Remo shouted. "There's nothing in there for you." There was silence aboard the rocket. "You heard me," Remo shouted. "Get down out of there. I'm going to slice you like a can opener."

He looked up at the open rocket hatch. He saw feet, and then with a light bound, Mr. Gordons dropped through the hatch and stood on the floor of the shaft, under the rocket, staring at Remo.

"Hello is all right. I thought you were not here."

"That's what you were supposed to think, you ambulatory adding machine."

"I would offer you a drink but I will not have time. I have to destroy you."

"You wish," said Remo.

"Is the yellow-skin here too?"

"Yes."

"Then I will destroy him too. Then I will always survive."

"You have to get past me first. I do all Chiun's light work," Remo said.

"For you, I will not use my simulated hands," Mr. Gordons said, and as Remo watched, the bones under Mr. Gordons's skin appeared to quiver, and then his hands rearranged themselves until they were no longer ten flesh-colored fingers attached to a palm, but two shiny steel knife blades jutting out from Gordons's wrist. Remo moved forward as if to attack. Inside the control room, Chiun hit the switch that lighted the window and it cleared in front of them, just in time to see Mr. Gordons raise both knife-hands up over his head and charge at Remo slashing

171

both blades back and forth through the air. Remo stopped and waited until Gordons was almost on him, then feinted left, moved right, and slid out from under the twin blades and was behind Gordons, looking at his back.

"Back here, tin man," he called.

Mr. Gordons turned. "That was a very efficient maneuver," he said. "Do you know that I now have it programmed? If you do it again, I will surely kill you."

"Well, then, I'll do something else."

Mr. Gordons moved toward Remo, this time moving the knife blades in front of him in large circles, as if he were conducting an orchestra with knives for batons.

Remo waited until Mr. Gordons closed the gap. Gordons lunged forward at Remo, who leaped up, put a foot on Gordon's shoulder and went up over the android's back a split second before the left knife blade flashed into that area. The blade missed Remo but bit deeply into Mr. Gordons's own mechanical left shoulder.

"Put that one in your program," Remo said from behind Mr. Gordons. "If you do that one again, you'll cut your own throat."

Mr. Gordons felt a strange sensation welling up in him. It was new; he had never felt it before. He paused to isolate it, but it would not let him pause. It was anger, cold, evil anger, and it forced hm to run forward toward Remo, who dodged between Gordons's legs and came up behind him, even while Gordons's own momentum slammed him forward into the steel wall lining the launch chute and the right knife blade snapped off and dropped with a heavy click onto the floor.

Mr. Gordons looked up over his head through the plastic window. There he saw Dr. Carlton, high probability Chiun, and someone he had never seen before. The sight of Dr. Carlton watching him fail raised his anger even higher. He turned again and charged Remo who stood lounging against the wall on the far side of the tube. Again Remo waited until Gordons was almost on him, then Remo spun fully around, vaulted up and grabbed one of the rocket supports high overhead, and swung over Mr. Gordons's head.

Gordons, in rage, swung his knifeless arm. The metallic stump thudded against Remo's calf with a loud sharp crack. Remo swung out of danger and dropped lightly to his feet, but when he landed, his left leg buckled under him and he fell to the floor of the rocket chute. He tried to scramble to his feet, but his left leg would not support him. The muscles had been damaged by the swing of Gordons's arm. Remo hoisted himself up, putting his weight on only his right leg, and turned to face Gordons again.

"You are damaged now," said Mr. Gordons. "I will destroy you."

And then, echoing through the chute with the sound of thunder came a voice that seemed beyond time and space.

"Hold, machine of evil."

It was the voice of Chiun, the Master of Sinanju. The door alongside the control panel was open and framed in it, wearing his red robes, stood the aged Oriental.

"Hello is all right," said Mr. Gordons.

"Goodbye is better," said Chiun. He leaped from the open doorway down into the bottom of the pit, and from the floor snatched up the foot-long blade that had broken off Mr. Gordons's arm.

173

"Now I will destroy you also," Mr. Gordons said.

He turned toward Chiun who backed slowly along the wall until he was on the opposite side from the open control room door.

"How will you destroy me when you have not creativity?" said Chiun. "I am armed with a weapon. Remo, the door."

Remo turned and pulled himself up, through the open door, dragging himself heavily onto the control room floor. As soon as he was inside, Smith slammed the door shut. Remo hobbled to the panel to watch the battle.

"It's terrible," Dr. Carlton said softly, to herself. "Like watching my father."

"I *am* creative," came Mr. Gordons's voice.

"I will attack you with this blade," said Chiun.

"Negative. Negative. You will simulate an attack with the weapon and then attack me with your open hand. It is a creative way. I understand creative ways."

He stood his ground, only eight feet from Chiun, looking at him.

"But I have thought of that," said Chiun. "I knew you would think that. And so, because you think the attack by blade will be false, I will truly carry it out. And the blade will destroy you."

"Negative, negative," Mr. Gordons shouted, his voice rising in angry desperation. "I know now your plan. I will guard against the attack by blade."

"I have thought of that too," said Chiun. "And because of that the true attack will come by my hand."

"Negative, negative, negative, negative, negative," shrieked Mr. Gordons. "Nobody is that creative. I am creative. Nobody can deceive me."

"I deceive you," said Chiun.

"And I destroy you," Mr. Gordons shouted, and

made the fatal mistake he was programmed never to make. He attacked first. His left knife blade swung before him. His eyes watched the blade in Chiun's right hand and, then darted to Chiun's open left hand, then back, again and again. And when he was almost upon Chiun, Chiun moved his open left hand away from his body and when Mr. Gordons's eye turned to follow it, Chiun hurled the knife blade forward from his right hand. It hit between Mr. Gordons's eyes and buried itself four inches deep. There was a shower of sparks as the metal cut through circuits inside Mr. Gordons's head and he screamed, "My eyes, my eyes, I cannot see."

And Chiun was over his fallen body, and he withdrew the knife from between Mr. Gordons's eyes, and then plunged it again into his chest. It sizzled and sparks flew as it cut even more wires and Mr. Gordons thrashed about spastically on the floor of the rocket chute, and Chiun looked up to the window where the three persons watched, and motioned for them to press the launch button.

Remo shook his head but Smith reached out and hit the red button marked "launch." The rocket tube was immediately filled with a roar like thunder. Flames belched from the bottom of the rocket, red, orange, yellow, and blue flames that poured down onto the stone floor of the tube and rebounded upward in droplets of fire. And under their blast lay Mr. Gordons and as they watched, they could see the clothing burn off him, then the pink plastic flesh melt, and then the mass of wire, tubes, transistors, and metallic linkages begin to glow red and flash into flame.

Chiun was not to be seen, but then with a blast of heat that seemed to come from the gates of hell itself, the control room door opened and Chiun leaped through, pushing the door shut behind him. He moved quickly to the window, arriving just in time to see the rocket quiver on its launch pad, then slowly lift itself up a few inches. It hovered there, motionless, and then began rising, lifting off with ever-increasing speed, its powerful thrusters screaming in the narrow confines of the launching tube, its flames brightening the shadowed area underneath itself, and then the shaft was sunlighted as the rocket cleared the tube and moved skyward.

At the bottom of the tube lay a small pile of electronic rubble, still simmering and smoking.

Remo looked toward Chiun.

"You were right," Chiun said. "He moved funny."

With a sob, Dr. Carlton turned from the control panel and ran from the room.

"How's your leg?" Smith asked Remo who sat on the control panel.

"It's coming back. The muscles were just stunned, I guess."

"Good, because there are still some things we have to do."

"Like what?"

"Like find Mr. Gordons's printing operation, and destroy his plates and paper supplies. We're in just as big trouble if someone else finds them."

Remo nodded. He turned to speak to Chiun.

But Chiun was not there.

Mr. Seagrams had just handed Dr. Carlton a martini when Chiun entered her office.

"You are a beautiful lady," he said.

She did not answer, instead staring at his cold hazel eyes, her drink frozen in her hand.

"You are also intelligent," he said. "You know why I am here, do you not?"

She gulped and nodded.

"Never again must Remo and I face such a challenge. Mr. Gordons came from your brain. No more such creatures must come from your brain."

She looked at his eyes again, tossed back her head and drained the martini in one swallow, then lowered her head for the blow.

Chiun's hand raised and came down just as Remo limped into the room.

"Chiun," he called. "Don't . . ."

But it was too late. The blow had already struck.

Remo ran forward to Dr. Carlton's side. "Dammit, Chiun, there are still things to do."

He knelt alongside Vanessa Carlton. "The printing plant, Vanessa," said Remo. "The plates, the paper, the press . . . where does Gordons keep them?"

She looked at Remo and a faint smile crossed her face. "Remo," she gasped. "He is . . . the . . ."

Vanessa Carlton died.

Remo lowered her gently to the floor and stood up. "Dammit, Chiun, we've got to find out where he kept his money plant."

"I do not care for money. I get paid in gold."

With a swirl of his robes, Chiun turned and walked from the room, Remo following after him.

In the corner of the room silently stood the pleasure android, Mr. Smirnoff. He watched as the two men left—the one who had given her such pleasure—then turned his head to look at Dr. Carlton's creamy white legs, exposed up to her hips, as she lay on the floor. Slowly, he began to walk toward her prone body, unzipping his trousers as he went.

177

That night, in Vanessa Carlton's living quarters, Remo found an envelope addressed to her. In the left corner over the imprinted legend "First Ranchers Trust Company, Billings, Montana," he saw the typewritten notation: "From Mr. G."

"That's it," he told Smith. "Someplace in this bank."

"Go there," said Smith. "I am returning to Folcroft."

Remo and Chiun walked through the rocket control room minutes later as they were leaving the laboratory. They looked through the plastic window down into the rocket shaft. Remo grunted with satisfaction, but Chiun was silent. Were his eyes playing tricks on him? Did the pile of rubble there seem smaller than it had nine hours earlier?

Chiun waited at the Billings Airport while Remo took a cab into town. The cabdriver told him that the First Ranchers Trust Company had gone out of business ten years earlier. "A lot of eastern hippies began moving here and the ranchers moved out. The bank closed its doors."

"Well, take me there anyway," said Remo.

It was midnight when the driver let him out in front of the old yellow brick building on the fringes of the town's business district. The windows had been covered over with wood, and metal plates covered the front door.

Remo waited until the cabdriver turned the corner, made sure no one was watching, then forced up the edge of one of the metal plates to expose the door lock. He slammed his hand against it, and the door quivered, then opened. Remo stepped inside the pitch blackness of the bank and closed the door behind him.

He was not alone.

He realized it. He felt it through his feet rather than his ears; there were vibrations in the bank. Something was moving. Someone already had found Mr. Gordons's operation. Or maybe he had had a partner? God, not another one, he hoped.

Remo moved through the blackness of the bank, following the vibrations. They took him down a back stairway to an underground level. In front of him stood a closed vault door. He moved toward it and paused. Behind it, he could hear vibrations, machinery working.

He waited, then pulled open the vault door. The vault was small and brightly lit from an overhead bulb. In the center of the floor stood a printing press; its motor was running and in front of it on the floor was a large pile of hundred-dollar bills.

But there was no one to be seen. Remo stepped inside the door, and checked on both sides. No one. The vault was empty.

He went to the far wall. Perhaps there was a secret panel. He didn't know anything about banks. Maybe vaults had secret panels behind which bankers stashed the real stuff, mortgages and bonds they had stolen from widows and orphans.

He ran his hands over the wall, looking for seams in the concrete. But there were none. Puzzled, he stood there momentarily. Then he heard a voice behind him.

"You have damaged me, Remo." It was Mr. Gordons's voice. But it couldn't . . . Remo wheeled. The printing press was moving itself through the door. There was no one or nothing else in the room.

The vault door closed. From outside, he heard Mr. Gordons's voice.

"You have damaged me but I will repair myself.

179

Then I will come for you and the yellow man. Like your House of Sinanju from whom I learned in combat, I will not allow you or your maker to survive."

Remo ran to the door and pushed but it was tightly sealed. "How did you survive?" he yelled.

"I am an assimilator," came Gordons's voice faintly from outside. "So long as one piece of me remains, it can rebuild the rest from whatever materials are near."

"But why did you turn yourself into a press?" called Remo.

"Dr. Carlton told me once, if you have money you will survive. I must survive, so I must make money. Goodbye, high probability Remo."

Remo put his ear to the door. He could hear a faint squeaking outside, as if machinery was being dragged along the floor. Then there was silence.

It took Remo two hours to remove the hinges of the vault door and to free himself. Before leaving, he set fire to the fresh rag content paper that stood clean, almost oily white, in the corner. The newly-minted hundred-dollar bills he stuffed into his shirt.

There was no one to be seen outside on the night-emptied streets of Billings.

He walked toward the few lights in the heart of town.

Sitting on the sidewalk in front of a newspaper office, he saw a bearded hobo wearing an old Marine shirt and a straw hat.

Remo took all the money from his shirt and dumped it at the hobo's feet. "Here," he said, "have a million dollars. I used to be a newspaperman myself."

"Only a million?" said the hobo.

"You know how it is," Remo said. "Money's tight just now."

Watch for

BRAIN DRAIN

next in the
AUTHORS' CHOICE BEST OF THE DESTROYER
series from Pinnacle Books

coming in June!